THE MIDNIGHT SEA

The Midnight Sea is an authentic account of life in the navy during the Second World War. When Hitler invaded Russia in the summer of 1941, Britain came to her aid with supplies and weapons. Since Germany controlled all the land routes, Britain was obliged to send her convoys by way of the Arctic Ocean to the north Russian port of Murmansk. Known as 'the Murmansk run', this phase of naval operations was full of hazard but vital to allied strategy. In this book we learn of life on the aircraft-carrier H.M.S. *Viper*—a life full of hardship and danger, yet rich with excitement and a sense of purpose. It is the first novel of a young New Zealander with first-hand experience of the scenes he describes.

UNICORN BOOKS

UNICORN BOOKS

General Editor: JAMES REEVES

★

IAN CAMERON

The Midnight Sea

Illustrated by
WINSTON MEGORAN

HUTCHINSON EDUCATIONAL

HUTCHINSON EDUCATIONAL LTD
178–202 Great Portland Street, London, W.1

London Melbourne Sydney
Auckland Bombay Toronto
Johannesburg New York

★

First published 1958
First published in Unicorn Books 1960

30437

This book has been set in Baskerville type face. It has been printed in Great Britain by The Anchor Press, Ltd., in Tiptree, Essex, on Smooth Wove paper and bound by Taylor Garnett Evans & Co., Ltd., in Watford, Herts

THE MIDNIGHT SEA

1

SNOW was falling over the islands of the Outer Hebrides. In the north it fell heavily; hard, brittle granules that beat like hail on to the decks of the ships in Stornoway harbour. But in the south it fell more lightly; softer, gentler flakes that turned to water the moment they settled on the braes.

By dawn the runways on Benbecula aerodrome were ankle-deep in melted snow.

The aerodrome itself was very still. Sodden, silent and apparently deserted, it lay in a miasma of water, cloud and mist. In the marshland between the runways, the flocks of dunlins and gulls, skuas and oyster-catchers slept close-packed: motionless as the flight of Coastal Command Wellingtons parked in front of the eastern hangars.

Quite suddenly the runway lights were switched on; the globes of orange-yellow, each with its refracted halo, shining like marsh gas through the mist. The birds stirred, shifted from one webbed foot to the other, fluffed up their feathers against the cold, and listened.

Down by the hangars an aircraft engine spluttered and coughed, faltered for a moment, then deepened into a pulsating roar.

The dunlins, skuas and oyster-catchers rose silently. In a great wave they passed through the golden light of the flares and flew noiselessly across the Sound to settle on Carinish and Grimsay. But the gulls were reluctant movers. Angrily they wheeled and mewed above the runways, settling at random on landing lights, wind sock and hangar roof.

7

Only when the aircraft taxied out to the runway did they wheel complainingly away.

It was a Swordfish aircraft that came splashing through the slush: a Mark IV Swordfish of 811 Squadron. In the pilot's cockpit Lieutenant-Commander Jago, the Squadron C.O., checked his trim, mixture, fuel and flaps as he taxied towards his point of take-off. In the observer's cockpit an insignificant little man with white hair, glasses and a diffident manner sat patiently on his parachute pack. Jago wondered if his queer little passenger knew how to adjust his safety harness.

'Are you strapped in, sir?'

'Yes. I've been strapped in some time.'

So it's true, thought Jago; you *are* in a hurry, and you're not as meek and mild as you look. He swung into wind and took-off quickly, in a flurry of mist and snow.

In the observer's cockpit Captain Hugh McInnes Jardine, O.B.E., D.S.O., R.N., peered into the darkness, thinking that in thirty years the Navy had given him some strange assignments but never one that had started as mysteriously as this. He looked at his watch—one of the old-fashioned pocket variety that told one not only the time but also the day, month and year: 7.30 a.m., Tuesday, December 2nd, 1944. Just twelve hours earlier he'd been sitting down to dinner at his home on the Sussex Downs; now he was circling the Outer Hebrides, in an open biplane, with the visibility down to zero. He hoped his pilot was capable of finding the rendezvous.

The Swordfish kept low. From fifty feet Jago could just make out the wrinkled carpet of the sea. For ten minutes he headed west; then he saw them; dead ahead; the shadows of warships darkening the mist. He flashed his recognition signal, and one of the ships—an aircraft-carrier—replied with the code letters of the day, and switched on her landing lights: twelve frosted stars outlining a diminutive deck.

Five minutes later Jago had landed-on, and Captain Hugh McInnes Jardine had clambered out of the Swordfish and taken over his new command.

8

He at once went below, down to his cabin, down to where he knew he'd find the key to the mystery: the carrier's sailing orders. The familiar oilskin packet, heavily sealed, was lying on top of his desk. He sat down and started to read, half prepared for an anti-climax. But the orders were anything but that.

.   .   .   .   .

Captain Jardine was a small, slightly built man, with an untidy mop of white hair (though he was only forty-nine), a firm mouth and gentle slate-grey eyes set unusually far apart. After he had read the orders he called a conference of senior officers.

The conference was held in the wardroom. When Jardine entered he was surprised to find the room practically full—he had never known a carrier with so much gold braid aboard. He could sense the expectancy as he walked across to the small table that stood by itself at the far end of the room.

'Sit down, gentlemen,' he said.

There was a scraping of chairs, then silence.

'Most of you,' he said—and his voice was pitched so low that those at the back of the room had to lean forward to hear what he was saying—'most of you came aboard the same way as I did. Secretly. At short notice. You'll have gathered then that we are a special team, brought together for a special purpose. I can now tell you what that purpose is.'

He paused. 'This carrier, gentlemen, will be flagship of a force that sails tomorrow to escort a convoy to Murmansk. I expect most of you have been to Murmansk before; probably you're wondering what all the fuss is about. The point is this. Our convoy is no ordinary one. In the ships we guard there'll be a specially vital cargo. The best thing, I think, would be for me to read you a few extracts from our sailing orders. Then you'll understand the importance of what we're going to do.'

9

He pulled out a sheaf of papers and laid them on the table. In the gently swaying wardroom his voice rose and fell for the greater part of an hour. Several times he referred to a chart of the Arctic; once or twice he drew tactical diagrams.

Leading Steward Wallace, with his ear glued to the serving-hatch that connected wardroom and galley, couldn't see the chart, and he could distinguish only an occasional word. But there was one word that he heard several times—Murmansk. It was not a word that pleased him.

'Stone the crows!' he muttered. 'A Roosian convoy. In the middle o' bluidy winter.'

Sucking his teeth in disgust he went below to the galley; and within an hour the news that the carrier was joining a convoy to Russia had percolated to every corner of the ship.

.   .   .   .   .

As soon as the conference was over, Jardine went on deck. For the last hour the carrier had been zig-zagging among the islands of the Hebrides. Two destroyers had been keeping station on either flank; one of her aircraft had been circling overhead. Now Jardine stood her northward, parallel to the Scottish shore.

Soon it stopped snowing. Here, close to the coast, the sea was calm, the sky was clear and the sun was shining palely. For the rest of the morning Jardine stayed on deck, watching the fairy-tale islands of the Hebrides drop gradually astern: Uist and Berneray, Scalpay and Fladdachain, Lewis and Skiant and Skye. Theirs was a fey, tempestuous beauty that never failed to delight him. Snow-white isles, with the tide-rip flowing darkly in between, like ink spilt into the sea. And as morning gave way to afternoon a panorama of even greater beauty unfolded on the carrier's beam; the snow-capped peaks of Sutherland and Wester Ross, wreathed in cloud, mounting the eastern sky in majestic disarray.

That afternoon Jardine got to know a little of his ship and crew.

H.M.S. *Viper* was a British-built escort carrier of 16,000 tons; she had recently been refitted in the Clyde and her equipment, Jardine soon discovered, was of the latest type. Her senior and technical officers had been hand-picked; several of them had served with Jardine before. And her combined Torpedo-Bomber-Reconnaissance and Fighter Squadron (equipped with Wildcats and Swordfish) went about their flying with the minimum of fuss and maximum of efficiency. And they'll need to be good, thought Jardine, to see us through to Murmansk.

All that day *Viper* stood to northward.

A little before three o'clock Jardine was watching the cliffs of Cape Wrath disappear into the evening haze, and thinking for no apparent reason of his son, when the Officer of the Watch came hurrying across the bridge.

'The S.M.O. would like to see you, sir. He says it's urgent.'

'Ask him to come up.'

A minute later the Senior Medical Officer clambered on to the bridge. He was a fair-haired R.N.V.R. commander: a Harley Street specialist before he joined the Navy.

'I'm afraid,' he said, 'I've bad news. An acute appendicitis: ought to be operated on at once.'

'Can't you operate?'

'That can be the least of your worries, sir. The man I've got to operate on is the senior batsman.'

Jardine shivered: chilled by a sudden premonition. A batsman is one of the most vital members of an aircraft-carrier's crew; without a first-class man to control the aircraft as they land-on, a carrier is hamstrung, for her planes cannot operate. They had, Jardine reflected, a tough enough mission without running into trouble before they even met the convoy. Restlessly he paced the bridge. How, with *Viper* already north of John o' Groats and sailing under strict radio silence, could they get a replacement batsman? Once his mind was made up he acted quickly.

A little after three o'clock *Viper* heeled sharply over as she altered course. Half an hour later she came, very fast, through the boom at Scapa Flow. Before she lost way, her signal lamps were flickering urgently.

.　　　.　　　.　　　.　　　.

Daylight was fading; and the Royal Naval air station of Hatston, at the edge of Scapa Flow, lay cold and silent, blanketed in fine powder snow.

The sudden cough of an aircraft engine rang out across the deserted aerodrome. Gradually, as the throttle was eased open, the cough deepened to a pulsating roar; little flurries of snow scudded out behind a solitary plane; a necklace of icicles, caught in the slipstream, cascaded off a hangar roof; and sea-birds rose in shrilling protest above the snow-packed runways.

In his office Captain Galbraith listened to the aircraft warming up. The throb of its engine drove him to deeper concentration. He turned again to the signal and the four dossiers laid out on his desk. For the signal, the dossiers and the aircraft warming-up were part of the same problem. The signal—a top priority one—was from *Viper*: 'SEND ME AT ONCE YOUR BEST, REPEAT BEST, BATSMAN' it read. The dossiers were the personal records of the four batsmen who happened to be in Hatston that afternoon. And the aircraft warming up was waiting to fly the man of his choice aboard the carrier.

But which man, Galbraith wondered, should he send?

The question, he knew, was an important one, not to be lightly decided. He had heard rumours of *Viper* and her hand-picked crew and specially trained squadron. Obviously she was off on some important mission. She would need a first-class man. His frown deepened as he studied the dossiers. They were not, he decided, a very impressive lot: an ageing lieutenant, posted to Hatston for a rest from operations; two sub-lieutenants, one recently trained and the other with no sea-going experience; and a young lieutenant who had flown into Hatston only the evening before. This last man seemed to Galbraith the most promising. He was a Swordfish pilot who a year ago had broken his leg, and had taken a batsman's course while temporarily grounded. Now fit again, he was qualified as both batsman and pilot. Here, Galbraith decided, was his first choice.

Ten minutes later the young lieutenant was shown into his office. He was a tall, slimly built man, with greying hair (though he was still in his early twenties), a large hooked nose, a sensitive mouth and wide-apart grey eyes. Galbraith handed him the signal.

'Would you like to go?'

The young lieutenant read the signal.

'Yes, I think I would.'

Galbraith studied him carefully, for some undefinable reason he suddenly wondered if his choice had been right.

'I'm not,' he said, 'ordering you to go. This is a special assignment: probably a dangerous one. If you don't like it, I'll find somebody else.'

'I should like to go, sir.'

'Right,' said Galbraith. 'I'll have you flown aboard.'

'I could fly myself.'

Galbraith considered him carefully.

'Very well. *Viper*'s pulling out of harbour now. A plane's ready. If you hurry, you'll reach her before it's dark.

.   .   .   .   .

A squall of snow was sweeping the tarmac as the young lieutenant walked across to his plane. The wind caught at his breath, the snow hammered at his eyes; but he forced himself to look upward into the darkening sky. To seaward the horizon was a dull ochre, streaked with ribbons of grey. Above the Flow a dark mass of cumulus hung poised over the anchored ships; and in the west a flaming segment of

13

sun dipped into the blood-red sea. The day was dying angrily.

He lowered himself into the open cockpit of the Swordfish. As if from very far away he heard the Petty Officer's voice.

'Your kit's in the back, sir. Good luck!'

Then automatically he started on his pre-flight check; easing the throttle forward, noting the r.p.m.; checking his oil and fuel; flicking down the magneto switches; finally he swung the control column in a gentle clockwise circle, kicked forward on either rudder-bar, and called up Flying Control. Permission to take off came crackling into his earphones. He waved away the chocks. Two riggers scrambled forward and jerked aside the wooden blocks; then they clung to his wingtip, helping to turn the plane crosswind on to the ice-coated taxi-track that led to the end of the duty runway. As he taxied across for take-off the Swordfish slipped and slithered on the ice.

At the approach to the duty runway he halted. From the Flying Control van a green Aldis flickered out of the gathering darkness. He swung the plane into wind, pulled down his goggles and, leaning forward, opened the throttle wide.

The plane surged forward. Almost at once her tail lifted and the runway came into view—a narrowing ribbon of hard-packed snow, its outline blurred in the twilight and half obscured by an approaching squall. He felt the plane swing suddenly as the wind struck her; correcting automatically with stick and rudder, he held her down, until at sixty-five knots she lifted cleanly into the turbulent air.

He knew then that there could be no turning back. An alien fear, a premonition of things to come, suddenly took hold of him. I was a fool, he told himself, to pretend I wanted to go. The devil was thrown out of paradise for pride.

Many people on Hatston aerodrome heard, above the blustering wind, the throb of a Swordfish taking off. A few of them looked up and saw the plane disappearing to seaward in a veil of driving snow. Mostly their feelings were impersonal and ended in a forgetful shrug; but beside the control tower a girl with dark hair and sea-blue eyes stood watching long after the plane had disappeared, and listening long after its engine beat had died. She felt suddenly cold.

The Swordfish climbed to five hundred feet, then headed out to sea. It was almost dark by the time the young lieutenant picked up *Viper*'s bow wave: a sliver of whiteness in the carpet of crumpled grey. Hearing the throb of his engine, the carrier had already switched on her landing lights and was swinging into wind. He saw the illuminated discs, controlled by the batsman, motioning him in to land. As always, the prospect of a carrier landing quickened his breathing; he felt the familiar pricking across the nape of his neck, the familiar sweat breaking out on his palms. He lowered his arrestor hook and concentrated on watching the bats. It's your life, he told himself, reflected in the illuminated discs.

As he dropped towards the carrier in a gentle, descending arc, the bats were steady; but when he straightened into the final approach one of them vanished. Gently he eased the throttle back; his speed dropped from sixty-five knots to sixty, and at once the bats reappeared, level and reassuring. Level and nearer—much nearer. Over his engine cowling he watched them streaking towards him. He saw them flash downward and together in the signal to cut his engine, he jerked back the throttle and held the stick central; then the blurred outline of the flight deck fanned out before him. With a spasm of relief he felt the plane land squarely; felt the savage jerk of the arrestor wire; felt all movement die, and heard, in the moment of silence as the plane lay motionless on the flight deck, the murmuring hiss of bow waves sliding past the carrier's hull.

He climbed out of the plane. From a group of officers standing in the shadow of the island, a small slightly built man came across the deck towards him. Even in the half-light he could distinguish the two-and-a-half straight rings,

15

the D.S.O., D.S.C. and bar, and the gold wings of a pilot. The Squadron C.O., he thought. They shook hands.

'Come on to the bridge,' the C.O. said. 'I'll introduce you to Commander Flying.'

They picked their way over the flattened arrestor wires.

Captain Jardine watched them as they crossed the deck. He leant forward. His hands tightened suddenly on to the deck rail. Quickly he left the bridge. As he hurried below he passed the Yeoman of Signals.

'Chief,' he said, 'tell the new batsman to report to my cabin. At once.'

The Yeoman's eyes flickered in interest.

'Aye, aye, sir.'

Now what, he wondered, can have bitten the Old Man? He looked as if he'd seen a ghost.

The young lieutenant felt only a mild surprise that the Captain should want to see him at once. He might have waited, he thought until I'd had some tea. Walking down the corridor that led for'ard from the wardroom he had no fear, no premonitions; but when he knocked on the Captain's door, and heard the well-known voice telling him to come in, the years rolled back. He opened the door, and saw his father standing with his back to the two-barred electric fire.

They talked together for an hour. They spoke of home, of their friends, of all that had happened since they had last seen each other; they spoke of the war; and lastly they spoke of the coming convoy.

'I'm afraid it won't be an easy one,' Captain Jardine said.

'Russian convoys aren't usually easy.'

The Captain sighed. 'I wish,' he said, 'they'd sent me any batsman but you—for your sake,' he added hurriedly.

His son flushed. 'I'm considered quite a good batsman,' he said.

'I didn't mean it that way.'

'I'll try not to let you down, sir.'

The old constraint grew up between them. For a while

they spoke, like strangers, of things that neither were interested in; then the Captain went back to the bridge, and his son to find some tea.

.   .   .   .   .

All that night *Viper* and her destroyer escort stood northward. They moved fast, making up for the two hours they had lost in Scapa Flow. Their bow waves stood out like swathes of light; their wakes shone phosphorescent; their decks glowed silver in the moonlight that came flooding down from a sky which was clear and cold.

And ninety miles to the north, in sea lanes guarded by mine-belts and patrolled by shore-based Liberators of Coastal Command, the merchantmen bound for Murmansk were beginning to assemble.

2

The sun rose next morning into a cloudless sky. The sea was calm as a dew pond, the air keen as a surgeon's knife. And it was cold; already the thermometer on the bridge was recording twenty-seven degrees of frost.

A few minutes after sunrise the convoy was sighted: a smudge of darkness on the northern horizon.

At first the vessels looked lost and anonymous; papiermâché silhouettes dwarfed by the immensity of sea and sky. But gradually the blurred outline of their hulls took on detail and individual shape. Challenge and recognition signals started to flash across the sunlit water, and soon *Viper* was easing into position in the centre of the waiting ships. Bells tinkled, screws threshed at the water and the convoy stood northward for Murmansk.

It was a small but well-ordered convoy that left the assembly box that morning. From *Viper*'s bridge Jardine surveyed the vessels whose safety in the days ahead lay in his hands. The merchantmen, he decided, were a good-looking lot: biggish vessels most of them, and new, but not too new. They kept good station in three parallel columns. They made no smoke. They could all make twelve and a half knots. The warships looked reliable; and he knew most of their commanders—men whose experience had been won in the hard proving-ground of the North Atlantic. They, too, kept station accurately, without fuss. In the centre *Viper* and her attendant destroyer; spaced out around the perimeter the cruisers, destroyers and corvettes; five miles ahead the fanned-out destroyer screen; three miles astern 'tail-end Charlie', a solitary corvette.

Throughout the morning Jardine stayed on deck, watching his ships slide effortlessly through a sea that was smooth as glass. Hour after hour they headed north, watched by a blood-red sun that crawled low along the horizon. Watched, too, by a shore-based Liberator of Coastal Command, a great unwieldy aircraft that circled low over the advancing ships, the sunlight glinting redly on her wings and fuselage.

And while the Liberator was providing air cover, *Viper's* pilots and observers were being briefed in the crewroom by Commander Stone, the Air Operations Officer.

Stone was a tall, good-looking man of indefinable age: at twenty he had looked thirty; at forty he would still look thirty. Suave and softly spoken, his manners were perfect as any Flag Lieutenant's, and he had the additional advantage of having brains.

He spoke quietly to the thirty-odd pilots and observers who formed the aircrew of 811 Squadron. He told them how important the convoy was; how much the top-secret equipment—'my unofficial guess is that it's some sort of Radar'—was needed by the Russians; how the powers-that-be suspected that German Intelligence had got to know the equipment was being sent, and how Hitler himself was said to have given orders for it to be stopped—at any price— from getting through.

'So if,' he said, 'the convoy is spotted, the Germans will throw everything they've got at us. Aircraft. Submarines. Surface forces. The lot. They won't mind what their losses are, as long as the convoy is sunk.'

He went on to explain that because of other commitments the Admiralty could give them no further help once the convoy was under way; if they got into trouble they must fight their own way out.

'And if it comes to fighting,' he said, 'the odds will be pretty heavily against us. I want you to look at this.'

He pinned a table of comparative forces on to one of the crewroom bulkheads.

SURFACE FORCES

Allied	German
1 aircraft-carrier	1 heavy cruiser
	(possibly the *Brandenberg*)
3 light cruisers	9–10 destroyers
8 destroyers	15–20 E-boats
	(operating at extreme range)
6 corvettes	

AIR FORCES

Allied	German
8 Wildcats	100–120 light bombers (Ju.88s)
	10–20 reconnaissance planes
	(Blom & Vosses)

SUBMARINE AND ANTI-SUBMARINE FORCES

Allied	German
14 destroyers and corvettes	25–35 submarines in Norwegian waters
15 Swordfish	25–35 submarines in transit to and from N. Atlantic

For several minutes the squadron digested this in silence. Then the C.O. knocked out his pipe.

'I'll lay three to one,' he said, 'that if the *Brandenberg* comes out we sink her.'

. . . . .

At noon the Liberator left the convoy to return to her base in the Shetlands. Jardine watched her dwindle to a pin-point of silver low on the southern horizon; then she disappeared. He knew then he was alone, beyond the range of any outside help; and alone he would remain for eight

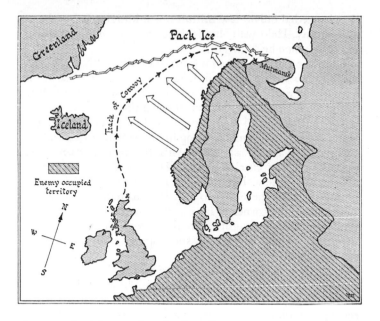

days and eighteen hundred miles, until Russian mine-sweepers guided his convoy into Kola Bay.

He watched the first of *Viper*'s anti-submarine patrols take off: an archaic-looking Swordfish, so festooned with depth-charges and specialized apparatus that she seemed scarcely able to stagger off the flight deck. From now until they reached Murmansk, these Swordfish would follow each other at two-hourly intervals. Circling the convoy in good weather and bad, in daylight and darkness, they would spot and hunt down any U-boat that surfaced within thirty miles of his ships.

All afternoon and evening the Swordfish patrols continued in easy succession. Jardine, wedged into his favourite corner of the bridge, knew the value of these uneventful hours; hours when the convoy was moving fast, and the miles that lay between them and their goal were swallowed with no apparent effort. He looked at his watch, and saw

21

that it needed only a few minutes to midnight. It had been a good day. He'd wait, he decided, for the next Swordfish to return; then he'd turn in.

Soon the throb of the plane came to him softly out of the night. *Viper* swung into wind; an Aldis lamp flashed from her bridge, and almost at once the grey ghost-like shadow of the Swordfish came floating toward them.

Jardine wondered if his son was doing the batting. He watched the plane come drifting in, off a shallow descending turn. She was almost level with the round-down now, poised over the carrier's stern. He sensed the batsman's satisfaction; knew that in a fraction of a second he'd be giving the pilot the signal to cut. He was half turning away when out of the corner of his eye he saw the plane suddenly flicker, as though caught in an air pocket. Her port wingtip dropped. Falling sideways, she toppled, out of control, straight for the catwalk.

A cry of fear rose thinly into the night. Gun crews flung themselves to the deck. But the batsman stood firm. The plane came lurching down on him. In the fraction of a second left him, he tried desperately to wave it to starboard, to align it centrally with the deck. And the pilot saw him; with a last-second flick of aileron and rudder he wrenched the Swordfish level, so that she landed safely, on the very edge of the flight deck. Her wingtip swept, at seventy miles an hour, over the batting platform. The batsman flung himself aside. But he was too late.

The lower wing, with a thud that was barely noticeable and did nothing to lessen the speed of the plane, smashed through his skull. He died as they were carrying him below.

.　　　.　　　.　　　.　　　.

In the warmth of his cabin Jardine poured out two glasses of whisky. He passed one to his son.

'I've been thinking, Ian,' he said, 'about what we can do to help you. One batsman simply isn't enough.'

'I'll be all right, Dad. Don't fuss!'

'The C.O. thinks that if you gave him a few lessons, he could try his hand at the daylight landings. That way you'd get some sleep.'

'Batting can't be learnt in a day.'

'No. But I think the C.O.'s got the only answer.'

Young Jardine flushed. 'You've never,' he said, 'had much faith in me, have you?'

'I'm not being personal.' The Captain got up and began to pace the cabin. 'I simply think the batting will be too much for one man—for any one man.'

'I can manage.'

Jardine looked at his son. I mustn't, he thought, destroy his confidence. I must keep my doubts to myself.

'Very well,' he said. 'If you're sure that's the way you want it. . . .'

'Thanks, Dad. I'm quite sure.'

They talked for several minutes of other things; then it was time for the next Swordfish to be landed-on, and young Jardine went hurriedly on deck.

He would, he realized, have little chance of rest in the next eight days. With the constant landing-on of patrols, he could never enjoy more than two hours' uninterrupted sleep; if the convoy ran into trouble he'd get no sleep at all. A whisper of doubt hovered at the back of his mind, but he shrugged it aside. It would be an opportunity, he told himself, to prove to his father that he had a son to be proud of. He collected his bats, and picked his way carefully over the flattened arrestor wires. Soon he heard the throb of the returning Swordfish, and saw the pale-blue navigation lights drifting toward the carrier's stern. He held his bats level, at 'Steady as you come'.

That night and the following day the convoy, moving fast through calm seas, headed north. The Swordfish patrols were uneventful, the Radar screen stayed blank. Soon the leading ships were crossing the 65th Parallel, only a hundred and fifty miles south of the Arctic Circle. It became steadily colder: a rating who laid his ungloved hand on the metal of a bofors gun had the skin of his palm

23

ripped clean away. It also became darker. The sun rose at ten now and set at two, and even at midday its rays were cold as starlight.

Young Jardine rigged up a bunk for himself in the crewroom. It was always dark in the crewroom (for aircrew going on patrol had to keep their eyes away from electric light); and he managed to cat-nap in between landings. He didn't, he told himself at the end of the second day, feel particularly tired; only a little muddled sometimes as he woke suddenly and found himself stumbling, still half asleep, on to his batting platform.

On the bridge Captain Jardine drank cup after cup of strong, sweetened tea. His face, as he watched his son moving uncertainly across the flight deck, was expressionless. That second night he stayed on deck until it was quite late, watching the flecks of cloud drift slowly past a haloed moon. At first the stars shone brightly into a metallic sky. But a little before midnight the flecks of cloud thickened and lowered; the stars paled; the moonlight weakened, and soon a snow-wet wind was sighing out of the west.

On his way below he called at the Met. Office. Carefully he studied the weather chart, and his lips tightened. He climbed into his bunk, fully dressed. The convoy, he knew, had started well, yet he was troubled. In his dreams he saw the close thick-pencilled circles of the weather chart darken into a fantastic stormcloud that came sweeping out of the west; while to the east, massed on the edge of darkness, lay a limitless Armada—U-boats close-packed stretching to the far horizon.

On the rucked-up linen sheet his fingers curled and twisted, and he woke in the silence of 3 a.m., trembling and damp with sweat.

3

I T W A S on the third day out that the convoy ran into trouble.

First, the weather. Throughout the early hours of the morning the wind increased, and the cloud thickened and lowered; at five o'clock the first squall of snow came lashing across *Viper's* flight deck; and soon the Swordfish were flying their patrols in a full blizzard, the snow as it struck the aircraft freezing into a thin veneer of ice. *Viper*, never at her best in rough weather, began to corkscrew uneasily.

A little before dawn young Jardine came sleepily on deck. *Viper* was just turning into wind preparatory to landing-on, and as she swung beam-on to the heavy seas she rolled sickeningly with a sideways-and-downward plunge that brought men's stomachs to their throats. Young Jardine found himself flung violently to the deck. Jerked very much wide awake, he grabbed an arrestor wire. The flight deck, he realized, had suddenly become a wild tempestuous place, with spume and spray skidding across an ice-coated deck. The night had grown suddenly darker; the sea had risen, and *Viper* was pitching heavily. Scrambling to his feet, he worked his way down deck. When he reached the batting platform he found that the carrier's stern was rising and falling by a full thirty feet. Landing the aircraft on wouldn't, he thought, be easy.

And he was right. Batting that morning was a test of skill and stamina and nerve. At the end of every landing he felt increasingly exhausted; mentally and physically. But he made no mistakes; the pilots obeyed his signals, and beside him plane after plane thudded safely down, their wheels slithering awkwardly on the ice.

At dawn the Captain came on to the bridge. Sheltered from the bitter wind, he watched his snow-veiled vessels pitching silently into the heavy head sea, great plumes of spray cascading over their bows and freezing into fantastic patterns on the iron decks. The storm, in spite of its growing violence, was not unwelcome to him; for it lessened the chances of the convoy being seen. He wedged himself more firmly into his corner of the bridge. If we're not spotted in the next forty-eight hours, he thought, we'll be as good as home.

But the next two patrols put paid, in no uncertain manner, to any hope of an uneventful trip.

.   .   .   .   .

Maitland and Sidwell took off a little after eight o'clock. Ted Maitland was one of the squadron's oldest and most experienced pilots; a solid, thick-set Cumbrian with two children and a blue-black beard. His observer, Johnny Sidwell, was a large round-faced young man, who laughed a lot, especially when he saw other people laughing.

When they were airborne they found it was too dark for them to make out either the sea or the ships of the convoy; so Maitland watched his instruments, keeping the plane level by his artificial horizon; and Sidwell concentrated on his A.S.V.X.—their air-to-sea radar-type equipment used for locating U-boats. The A.S.V.X. was not working well. Its screen flickered with distorted shapes and echoes. Interference, thought Sidwell; probably from electronics in the air. He gave the set a peevish clout. It flickered in protest; then its screen seemed to clear and a dark mass of echoes swam plainly into view. There, he told himself, is the convoy. Now to circle it. He flicked on his radio.

'Ted,' he called. 'Steer 095°.'

The plane banked to starboard, turning on to its new

course; and as it turned it sideslipped into a little air pocket. Sidwell's chart-board clattered to the floor; when he picked it up he failed to notice it was upside-down. And on that, the fate of the convoy turned.

For two hours Maitland and Sidwell circled the patch of echoes, which remained clearly in the centre of their screen. After two hours, their patrol finished, they turned into the centre of the area they had been circling. They expected to find the convoy easily, for it was getting light; but of the vessels they thought they had been circling there was no sign; they saw no smudges of smoke, no bow waves, nothing but a frightening emptiness of wind and sea and sky. Somehow the convoy had vanished, and they knew that unless they found it they would die.

They began a square-search. And almost at once Sidwell's eyes, like mercury to a magnet, were drawn to his radio. It would be so simple to call the carrier for a homing. So simple, but so disastrous. For if Sidwell used the radio, even for a couple of seconds, he knew what the price would be: his transmission would be picked up by listening posts along the Norwegian coast; the Germans would put two and two together and the secret convoy would be no secret any more. He moistened his lips, and for the fifth time checked his navigational plot. It never occurred to him that his mistake was as simple as having his chart-board upside down.

The sky grew lighter; but the cloud remained heavy and low, and visibility was never more than a couple of thousand yards. They covered a fair-sized area in their search—some sixty to seventy square miles—but there was no sign of the convoy; and to the steady throb of the Swordfish engine, the minutes, their petrol, and their expectation of life drained inexorably away. It was all the harder because they had so much time to think. All the harder because both knew that by switching their radio to transmit for perhaps five seconds they could save their lives.

After about an hour the engine spluttered and coughed, and Maitland switched on to the reserve fuel tank. They knew then that they had less than twenty minutes to live.

Sidwell felt little rivulets of sweat trickling from under his armpits. His mouth was dry. His heart fluttered like an imprisoned bird. The fluttering was more than he could bear.

'Ted!' he called.

'Yes?'

'We've only one chance. I'll call *Viper*.'

'No. We can't do that.'

It was said so simply and so finally that there was no room left for argument.

Men who are not themselves congenitally brave can sometimes draw courage from the strength of others. Sidwell unhooked his Very pistol, and with its barrel smashed the transmitting switch off the face of his radio.

They flew on in silence; anything they said seemed so very trivial now. Eventually the engine spluttered and cut dead.

Ted Maitland was a good pilot. But the sea was rough, and the plane ditched heavily. They managed to scramble out of the fuselage before it sank, but the wing containing their rubber dinghy broke off and drifted away before they could reach it. They watched it for several minutes, bobbing merrily from wave-crest to wave-crest; then it dipped out of sight. For a little while their mae-wests kept them afloat, but the water was very cold, and they did not live for long.

. . . . .

In *Viper*'s Operations Room Jardine and Stone stood watching the radar screen. On it they saw the Swordfish, a lonely pin-point of light that instead of circling the convoy went spiralling away to the south. Jardine felt slightly sick.

'Where,' he said, 'does he think he's going?'

Stone looked at the weather chart.

'I'm afraid he's following a cloud, sir. An electric cloud can make an echo on A.S.V.X. that looks very like a group of ships. He must be circling a cloud instead of the convoy.'

'There's not much hope for him, is there?'

'No.'

'Will he use his radio?'

'I should say probably not.'

Jardine picked up a cloth, walked across the Operations Room, and wiped Maitland's and Sidwell's names off the list of aircrew.

'The convoy's unprotected,' he said. 'Fly off another Swordfish.'

·   ·   ·   ·   ·

The convoy was without its patrolling plane for less than a quarter of an hour. But in that time the mischief was done. For fifteen miles ahead of the convoy a U-boat had broken surface.

And so as soon as the next Swordfish became airborne, a small pear-shaped blip appeared on the screen of its A.S.V.X. For several seconds the Swordfish observer stared at it in disbelief. (Things were happening too fast for him. Ten minutes ago he and his pilot had been sitting in the warmth of the crewroom playing liar dice; now, it seemed, they were about to plunge into an Arctic U-boat hunt.) He flicked his radio to intercom.

'Jock! There's an echo dead ahead. Range ten miles. Looks like a sub.'

Jock MacArthur swore softly. The U-boat couldn't have surfaced at a more awkward time or place; in the few minutes that the convoy had been unguarded she had managed to take up—by accident or design—an ideal scouting position. Soon she'd pick up the advancing vessels on her hydrophones; soon she'd be calling up her base with the news that a convoy was at sea. The convoy had only one chance, it seemed to MacArthur, of avoiding discovery. They must sink the U-boat. And sink it quickly.

They decided to go straight in.

In the low cloud and the heavy driving snow their target was invisible to the human eye. But the eye of the A.S.V.X. picked it out with startling clarity: the one pin-point of light in a thousand square miles of sea. Steering a succession of courses called through by his observer, MacArthur skirted the U-boat, manœuvring into a position from which he could attack down-wind. It took them ten precious minutes to get into position; then, with a thirty-five-knot wind behind them, they swept in to the attack.

Visibility was poor; and MacArthur, as he peered over his engine cowling, could see little except the dark veils of snow, pelting seaward out of the banks of cloud. He could only trust his observer's courses, and try to steer them accurately. Every few seconds these courses came crackling into his earphones.

'Course 160°. Range four miles.'

A squall of snow plastered across his windshield.

'Course 170°. Range three miles. Can't you see her yet?'

'I can't see a damn thing.'

'Course 165°. Range two miles.'

Then, over the rim of his engine cowling, he saw her; a sliver of metallic grey, dwarfed by the immensity of sky and sea.

'I've got her,' he cried, 'dead ahead. Reckon she hasn't seen us.'

But even as he spoke a thin ribbon of tracer swam slowly up. It seemed at first to leave the U-boat in a gentle, almost lazy stream; then as it neared them it accelerated sharply, until with a vicious crack it flashed beneath their starboard wing. The U-boat, it seemed, had no intention of diving; she was staying to fight it out. MacArthur knocked his depth-charge switches to 'live', and tipped the Swordfish into a shallow, corkscrewing dive.

Twice, in five-second bursts, tracer spat around them; the first stream passed a little to starboard, the second well to port. Then a long steady burst came directly at them. MacArthur crossed his controls; the Swordfish sideslipped violently; the wind tore sideways into the cockpit, and the tracer streaked inches below them. When they straightened out they were less than three hundred yards from the

U-boat. MacArthur reached for his depth-charge release button.

Then the rockets hit them.

Watching the U-boat grow larger in his sights MacArthur saw a sudden burst of flame from aft of her conning tower. A second later a salvo of blazing meteors tore into the plane. He realized, too late, that the U-boat was equipped with the latest rocket-type ack-ack. The Swordfish shuddered as three thirty-pound rocket heads splintered her starboard wing; she toppled seaward. Desperately MacArthur wrenched her level and aimed her straight at the U-boat. He saw the tracer coming again, flickering straight at his eyes. He tried to sideslip, but the plane no longer answered her controls. He felt her jerk and shudder as a hail of explosive bullets smacked into the engine. An artery of glutinous oil pulsated out, splintering the windshield, cascading into the cockpit. He was still trying to hold the plane on course when the rockets hit her again, ripping into her belly, toppling her seaward.

A ribbon of pain seared through his arm. He saw the horizon cartwheel crazily; saw the dark silhouette of the U-boat toppling out of his sights. He jabbed at his release button. The four depth-charges plummeted seaward. Then the Swordfish hit the water. She hit it obliquely, along the reverse crest of a wave; and as luck would have it she hit it flat, with the smooth under-surface of her lower wing (her undercarriage had been shot clean away). She bounced a full two hundred yards from wave-crest to wave-crest; then, a quarter of a mile from the U-boat, she belly-flopped into the sea. Spirals of steam from her burning engine rose into the air; and almost at once she began to sink.

MacArthur was dazed by the impact of ditching. His left arm hanging uselessly, he fumbled with his safety harness as the water came swirling into the cockpit. He had just worked himself free when the depth-charges detonated. Four mushrooms of water heaved skyward a little in front of the U-boat. Underwater waves, like ripples from a stone thrown into a pond, pulsated outward. Caught in these, the

Swordfish rocked violently; her nose dipped under, and in a little vortex of churned-up sea she sank. But in the few seconds before she went under MacArthur's observer had freed their dinghy, and into its inflating folds he dragged his half-conscious pilot. Panting, sodden and half frozen, they huddled together on the sea-wet deck-boards.

The dinghy spun about uneasily; it shipped vast quantities of water; every few seconds the ice-cold waves came flooding over their gunwale. But at last the observer managed to tip out their drogue anchor; the dinghy turned head into sea and began to ride more easily.

Then they remembered the U-boat.

MacArthur spotted her first; still on the surface, about a third of a mile away. It was impossible to tell from where they were how badly—if at all—she was damaged; but she seemed to be moving slowly, and her deck was crowded with men. Several of the men were clustered round something that looked like a gun; and it seemed to MacArthur as if the barrel was being swung towards them.

.   .   .   .   .

After the depth-charges hit the water there was a second of silence; the roar of the plane, the clatter of tracer and the flare and crack of rockets died simultaneously away; and in the sudden quiet the U-boat crew heard the gentle slap of waves swirling against their sea-wet deck.

Then the depth-charges detonated. They burst too far in front of the U-boat to destroy her, but near enough to cripple her. A deluge of spray swept her deck. She rocked violently. Two of her gun-crew lost their footing and fell into the churned-up sea; only one clambered back. A section of her armour-plating buckled slightly; a thin trickle of water seeped into her hull, and her port screw twisted out of alignment.

As the fountains of spray subsided, the U-boat captain stumbled aft to the conning tower.

'Leutenant Bruckner!' His voice rose loud and harsh in

the silence that followed the explosions. 'Call Trondheim. Tell them a carrier is at sea. Tell them——'

There was a sudden commotion at the base of the conning tower, and a seaman covered in oil forced his way on deck. His eyes were frightened.

'Herr Kapitan!' He wiped the oil from his mouth. 'The aft torpedo bay is flooding fast.'

Ten minutes later when they had assessed the damage, they found that the U-boat could neither dive, hold course, nor make full speed. She could move only along the surface, very slowly, in a wide erratic circle. She was still on the surface when her hydrophones picked up the destroyers of the advanced screen. Her captain knew then that this was his last voyage. As he stood irresolute, a seaman plucked at his arm.

'Herr Kapitan!' He pointed to the dinghy. 'I think they are just within range.'

The same thought had evidently crossed the mind of one of the U-boat's gun-crew, a thickset, bearded seaman who had heaved the machine-gun off its high-angle mounting and was setting it up on deck. The captain looked first at the dinghy, then at the seaman; the man's eyes as he squinted through the gun-sights were dark with anger. For a moment the captain was undecided; then he moved quickly across to the machine-gun and knocked its barrel aside.

'No,' he said. 'Let them be.'

It was a few minutes after this that the U-boat was picked up by a destroyer of the advanced screen. Soon three warships were bearing down on her as she limped at a knot and a half among the white-crested waves. The U-boat fought savagely, but without hope; the destroyers had little difficulty in sinking her by gunfire at a range of eleven hundred yards. But by then her radio had been transmitting for a good quarter of an hour; and at several listening posts along the Norwegian coast her signals had been picked up.

Throughout occupied Norway wires hummed across

mountain and fjord with the news that a carrier was at sea. Top-priority telephone messages were passed between Berlin, Berchtesgarten and the Norwegian High Command, and soon the Station Commander at the newly built German aerodrome at Mosjoen received a personal signal from the Führer.

'If the carrier escorts a convoy,' the signal read, 'every ship is to be obliterated. No matter what the cost.'

The Station Commander picked up his telephone.

'Leutenant Weilen!'

'Yes, Herr Commandandt?'

'How many planes have we on the convoy search?'

'Three. And three standing by.'

'Widen and intensify the search. Put on another nine planes.'

'But Herr Commandandt! We only——'

'That is an order, Leutenant.'

He smiled as he put the telephone down. Knowing the forces at his disposal he had every confidence that the Führer's order would be carried out.

· · · · ·

After the destroyers had sunk the U-boat they spent some time searching among the flotsam for survivors. They picked up seven—two of whom were wounded; they also collected some interesting pieces of wreckage which they thought might intrigue the experts.

They were about to return to the convoy, when they spotted the Swordfish dinghy.

A destroyer came quickly alongside. Ropes were thrown; and after several attempts a three-inch manila line fell flush across the dinghy's bow. But the men who lay huddled on the deck-boards never moved: not even when another line fell directly across them. The destroyer crew thought they must be dead. But when a boat had been lowered, and the men hauled into it, it was found that they were not dead (though very near to it); they were unconscious and frozen

35

literally stiff. Their clothes had to be cut away from them; and for several hours their lives hung in the balance. But in the warmth of the destroyer's sick bay they eventually thawed out. That night their breathing became stronger, and the blood flowed back into their limbs. Within forty-eight hours they were sitting up in their bunks, drinking a mixture of broth and rum; and after that their recovery was only a matter of time. For several days MacArthur expected to lose his arm, which had been shattered by tracer and now threatened to turn gangrenous; but in the end the arm too was saved. So they survived: two of the few members of 811 Squadron who lived to see the Russian shore.

.   .   .   .   .

Jardine moved restlessly about the bridge. Gone were the sunlit hours of yesterday; gone was his optimism. Within an hour, two of his aircraft had been lost; his convoy had been discovered; and the weather was deteriorating fast. He remembered his dreams; a sense of prophetic foreboding came suddenly over him. He decided to broadcast to the ship's company.

'Attention! Attention!' The Master at Arms' voice grated into the tannoy, and a moment later Jardine was broadcasting to the ship.

'I think it likely,' he said, 'that the Germans have got to know we are at sea. We must therefore expect to be attacked at any moment by either U-boats or aircraft, and I'm bringing the carrier to first-degree readiness.

'As you know, we've been entrusted with the protection of a very special convoy. What happens to it in the next few days will depend very largely on the skill and devotion to duty of this ship's company. I know I can rely on every one of you to pull his weight.'

The tannoy clicked off; and over the carrier there settled an uneasy silence, broken only by the dull roar of the increasing wind and the thud of *Viper*'s bows as she pitched into the mounting head swell. Through the short arctic

36

day and well into the night the carrier remained on the alert. Her lookouts scanned the lowering horizon with extra vigilance, her radar and asdic sets were tuned with special care. But the enemy never came.

As soon as the U-boat had been reported, Jardine altered the convoy's course, and increased speed in an effort to clear the area likely to be searched. And when by nine o'clock that evening no attack had developed there were some who thought that the danger had passed. Jardine did not agree. In spite of the thirty-knot wind and the squalls of driving snow, he kept his Swordfish circling the convoy. Not until midnight did he return the ship to normal routine; and even then he kept an anti-submarine patrol in the air.

Flying in such conditions was a calculated risk. But better, thought Jardine, have one or even two planes crash on landing than have the convoy surprised by a pack of U-boats. He realized that if a plane did crash, it might easily kill his son. This knowledge turned each landing into a special sort of hell; but it in no way affected his decision to keep his planes in the air.

The hours passed. The planes took off; they circled the carrier; they landed-on. Landing wasn't easy. One plane shattered her oleo leg and slewed half across the flight deck. Another missed the first five arrestor wires, and was only jerked to a halt by the sixth, within inches of the barrier. But there was no serious accident.

Eventually Captain Jardine went below. Fully dressed, he climbed into his bunk. He twisted the voice-pipe from the Air Operations Room to within a few inches of his ear, and tried to will himself to sleep. But sleep didn't come easily; and even when he did at last drift into semi-oblivion, his dreams were troubled, were haunted by the throb of Swordfish returning, like moths to a candle, to *Viper*'s flight deck. There were too many of them for his son to land. The sweat gathered across his forehead, then ran in little droplets into his mouth.

. . . . .

Hour after hour, in high wind and heavy squalls of snow, the planes circled the convoy. Each patrol was as uneventful as the last. Hour after hour the aircraft and U-boat plots lay empty side by side; and next to them the radar screen flickered white and empty, like the panel of a badly tuned television set. But in the small hours of the morning there crawled on to the radar screen a tiny pinhead of light. It appeared first in the bottom right-hand corner; then very slowly it began to edge towards the centre. Stone watched it for a couple of minutes, then reached for his voice-pipe.

The Captain answered at once.

'What is it, Ops?'

'Unidentified aircraft, sir. Heading directly for us.'

'What's the range?'

'Fifty to fifty-five miles.'

'I'll be up.'

4

JARDINE and Stone stood watching the radar screen. On it the pinpoint of light—the image of the searching aircraft—edged slowly toward the convoy. To start with it seemed as if the plane might pass a little ahead of the ships; but when it was about ten miles distant it altered course and headed more exactly toward them. Stone clicked his tongue.

'He's seen us,' he muttered.

Jardine nodded.

Five minutes later the point of light hung motionless in the centre of the radar screen. Jardine and Stone looked at each other. All their care, all their secrecy, had been in vain. The convoy was discovered.

A telephone tinkled faintly and Jardine picked it up.

'Yes?'

'Bridge here, sir. Enemy aircraft directly overhead.'

'Can you see her?'

'No, sir. She's above cloud.'

'Tell the First Lieutenant I'll be up.'

On deck it was numbingly cold, with a blustering north-west wind. The duty watch, as they stamped their feet and flexed their half-frozen toes and fingers, could hear high above them the syncopated beat of aircraft engines. They knew that through breaks in the cloud the German pilot would be counting the ships in the convoy, identifying the warships of the escort, reporting back their position, course and speed. And there was nothing they could do about it. For *Viper* had no night fighters.

Jardine clambered on to the bridge. Together he and the First Lieutenant stared at a sky that vibrated with the mocking beat of engines. Both knew that unless their shadower was shaken off the convoy was in for trouble.

There seemed little chance of losing her; but at least, thought Jardine, they could try. He watched the sky, and after about ten minutes ordered an alteration of course. One after another the merchantmen and warships heeled over and headed for a patch of moonlit sea that lay beneath a rift in the cloud. As they moved out of the shadows, each vessel in turn became bathed in silver light. Their gun crews stood by expectantly as above them drifted an expanse of open sky. But the aircraft saw its danger; its engine beat deepened, and increasing speed it forged ahead, avoiding the clear sky and taking cover on the fringe of a distant belt of cloud. From there it continued to shadow the convoy.

Jardine sighed.

An hour later they passed under a mass of low, especially heavy, cumulus. Again Jardine ordered an alteration of course; again the ships turned. This time they ran downwind, close-packed beneath the rolling folds of darkness. But the belt of cumulus was not wide enough to hide them; the shadowing aircraft crisscrossed it, and observed them first from one edge then from the other. The third time the plane passed overhead, the *Atalanta*, the only warship of the escort equipped with radar-controlled ack-ack, opened up with sighting tracer. Guided by the golden flecks that stabbed skyward, every vessel fired a blind half-minute burst into the cloud. The barrage was more noisy than effective; its only result was that their shadower—a Blom and Voss flying-boat from Mosjoen—became more cautious. It climbed to nine thousand feet, and veered off behind a cloud-bank. From there, like a hovering vulture, it continued to watch the convoy. And back to its base it passed a steady stream of reports. Soon the convoy had no secret left: its course, its speed, its composition; all had been radioed back to the German High Command.

Restlessly, Jardine paced the bridge. O, he thought, for a single night fighter! Just for half an hour. He brought *Viper* into wind to land a returning Swordfish.

He had been so preoccupied with trying to shake off the shadowing aircraft that he had quite forgotten his son. The sight of the hunched-up figure as it stumbled across the flight deck was like the probing of a knife at some forgotten wound.

But he needn't have worried. For young Jardine was not—as yet—in particular need of sympathy. He was a man with a great deal of nervous energy, and this, coupled with his determination to prove himself to his father, kept tiredness for the time being at bay. But the tiredness, although he did not realize it, was there, mounting at the back of his brain like flood water behind a dam. Already the strain and the lack of sleep were beginning to tell, and he was landing the planes automatically, in a semi-conscious haze. Because he was a good batsman and the pilots were good pilots, this for the present was enough; but it meant that he was ill-equipped to deal with an emergency.

After he had landed the Swordfish he stayed on deck, chatting for several minutes to the cat-walk gun crews. All the time they were talking they could hear, throbbing among the belts of cloud, the unnerving beat of the flying-boat's engines. The knowledge that every move they made was being watched and reported made them feel vulnerable, defenceless. Soon they heard the rumble and hiss of the lift. Another Swordfish, young Jardine thought, being brought on deck. But he was wrong. Out of the hangar there emerged not the Emmett-like outline of a Swordfish but the squat bulk of a Wildcat. For several seconds young Jardine stared at the Wildcat as though it were some strange and unfamiliar insect; then the significance of its coming on deck seeped slowly into his brain. Muttering to himself he hurried below.

In the crewroom he found Lieutenant Maybank, the Senior Fighter Pilot, clipping on an oxygen mask. Watching him was the C.O. They were arguing.

'It's not worth it,' Marsden was saying, 'you wouldn't stand a chance.'

Maybank went on testing his oxygen mask.

'And you can stop fiddling with that. I shan't let you go.'

Maybank grinned.

'I've already seen the Old Man,' he said.

Marsden turned away. He knew the near-impossibility of night-flying a fighter without specialized instruments; he knew the fallibility in darkness of human eyesight and judgment; he knew how difficult it would be for Maybank to sight, let alone shoot down, the shadowing aircraft; and he knew that even if he did manage to shoot it down he would stand very little chance of landing-on. He appealed to young Jardine.

'Don't you agree, Bats,' he said, 'it's a crack-brained scheme? All the odds are against it.'

'Yes,' said young Jardine. 'Like Thermopylae.'

.　　　.　　　.　　　.　　　.

From his plane ranged on the extremity of the flight deck Maybank looked into the darkness and was afraid. He could see nothing. He was annoyed to find he was trembling and his mouth was dry. But as *Viper* dropped astern of the convoys and began to swing into wind, his trembling stopped. An Aldis lamp flashed from the bridge.

He eased the throttle open until the plane hung quivering against her brakes. Then he released her. She leapt forward. The blurred outline of the flight deck tilted into indeterminate focus. Beyond it was solid blackness. Fear pricked up the hair on Maybank's neck, as at eighty knots the plane tore skidding down the deck. He missed the island by a couple of feet, plummeted over the bow, then rose in a screaming climb toward the stars. His eyes flickered desperately from instruments they could not read to the darkness they could not penetrate. He felt the Wildcat begin to tremble. Realizing she was about to stall, he

42

jerked the stick forward. Too far forward. Seconds later the controls stiffened; the plane was screaming seaward in a tight spiral turn. He blacked out as he managed to level off, only fifty feet from the sea.

For ten desperate minutes he fought to master the Wildcat. Then very gradually, and more by instinct than skill, he began to bring her under control. Slowly, as his eyes grew accustomed to the dark, the night took on a recognizable shape. Beneath him he saw a glint of silver moonlight reflected on the sea. Ahead, the deepest grey took on the outline of a heavy mass of cumulus. To starboard he recognized the lighter grey as open sky, shot with anaemic stars. By shining a torch on to his instrument panel he saw he was climbing northward, coming up to seven thousand feet. He turned on his oxygen.

In *Viper*'s Fighter Direction Office the tracks of the fighter and the seaplane were plotted with exact precision. As soon as he saw the Wildcat was under control, the F.D.O. called Maybank up.

'Hullo Jaybird One. Treetop calling. How much can you see?'

'Hullo Treetop. Not very much.'

'Hullo Jaybird. Can you steer a course?'

'Hullo Treetop. I can try.'

'Hullo Jaybird. Steer 010°. Keep climbing to angles ten.'

In a gentle arc the Wildcat turned on to her new course, and a few minutes later Maybank levelled off. He was flying away from the convoy now, parallel to a cloudbank that slanted away towards the haloed moon. Soon the F.D.O. called him again, telling him to turn to starboard on to another course. And almost as soon as Maybank had acknowledged the call, the F.D.O.'s voice again crackled into his earphones.

'Hullo Jaybird. Watch eleven o'clock low. Bandit is 1,000 feet below you, down-moon, flying on the same course.'

He peered over his engine cowling. Down-moon he could see more, much more: a ghostly panorama of cloud upon cloud rolling in magnificent disorder towards the southern horizon. But a little beneath him was a layer of strato-cumulus: folds of swirling grey. He reached for his mouth-piece.

'Hullo Treetop. There's cloud below me. I won't be able to see her.'

The reply was reassuring. 'Keep looking,' the F.D.O. said. 'The cloud will break soon.'

For several minutes he flew on, his eyes watering with the strain of probing the layers of stratocumulus. Then, quite suddenly, the cloud started to disperse; first it thinned out, then it broke into little fragments, like puffs of cigarette smoke.

'Hullo Jaybird.' The F.D.O.'s voice rose in excitement. 'You'll see her any second now.'

Maybank leaned out of his cockpit. You're optimistic, he thought. He peered over his cowling. All he could see were the patches of pearl-grey cloud scudding backward beneath his plane. Then suddenly across one of the patches a dark, ill-defined shadow floated into view. He realized it was the silhouette of the flying-boat, outlined against the moonlit cloud. A second later he saw the aircraft itself. He was surprised how small and unsubstantial it looked: a ghost-plane wandering the midnight sky.

Watching the plane carefully, he flicked his gun-button to 'fire', and eased the Wildcat into a shallow dive. From above and astern he closed with the unsuspecting aircraft. Two thousand yards, one thousand, five hundred; then the shadow came drifting into his gunsight. Gently his thumb tightened on to the firing-button.

The Wildcat shuddered with recoil. Cannon-shell and tracer ripped into the flying-boat's wing, then splayed diagonally across her hull. Like a string-jerked marionette the German toppled sideways, then banked into a tight turn. In the diffused moonlight distances were hard to judge, and as Maybank followed her into the turn his tracer flashed a fraction outside her sharply canted wing. He wrenched the Wildcat into a tighter turn. The plane suddenly shuddered. Realizing she was about to stall he

44

eased her level, and the flying-boat toppled out of his sights. It was half a minute before he spotted her again; she was a thousand feet below, streaking for cloud. He kicked the Wildcat into a thirty-degree dive. His hand froze on to the firing-button; and again cannon and tracer ripped into the German's hull. Maybank blacked out as, still firing, he pulled out of the dive.

When he regained consciousness a torrent of jet-black smoke was curtaining off the moon, and the flying-boat was spinning crazily toward the sea. Torch-like banners of flame were streaming out of her engines. She struck the water awkwardly. Her torn-off wings were flung high into the air, and for three-quarters of a mile her fuselage jerked and cartwheeled along the crests of the waves. Then her fuel tanks burst. Petrol was spewed out; and flames of indigo and blue leapt out of the burning sea.

Maybank shut his eyes. There, he thought, but for the grace of God, go I.

Flying back to the carrier he felt no elation, no satisfaction. The burning sea haunted his memory. He felt cold, depressed and desperately tired. He was flying the Wildcat almost carelessly now; twice he found himself wandering off course, once he stalled and nearly flicked into a spin. But when he reached the convoy and saw the landing lights of the carrier he managed to force himself back to a state of keyed-up concentration.

It was snowing hard as he flew low over the carrier. He was told to circle until the weather cleared. The delay frayed at his nerves.

It also frayed at young Jardine's.

From his batting platform he could hear the harsh staccato beat of the Wildcat's engines; but of the plane itself there was no sign. At last the snow eased off. *Viper* swung into wind; young Jardine picked up his bats; and the damage control ratings and the asbestos-coated fire-fighters came crowding into the catwalks. The carrier was very quiet, as slowly out of the night the Wildcat came drifting in. It was as if the ship herself was holding her breath.

45

Twice Maybank approached too low and too fast; and twice Jardine had to wave him off. Then came another flurry of snow. The strain was beginning to tell on young Jardine. He stood on the exposed batting platform, shivering; his bats hung inertly; snow plastered the back of his neck; the sweat on his forehead froze into little globules of ice. This can't, he thought, go on; next time I'll have to get him down. And as if his prayer had been answered, Maybank's third approach was better.

To Captain Jardine, watching from the bridge, it seemed right up to the last fraction of a second that the miracle was going to happen. He saw the plane come drifting in off a shallow descending turn. Soon she was almost level with the round-down, poised over the carrier's stern. He sensed his son's satisfaction, knew that any second now he would be giving Maybank the signal to cut. Then out of the corner of his eye he saw the plane suddenly flicker, as though caught in an air pocket. He saw her port wingtip drop. He saw her fall straight on top of the batting platform. He flung an arm across his eyes.

There was a shout of fear. Gun crews and handling party dived for the deck. Young Jardine saw the Wildcat come tumbling out of the sky. Dropping his bats, he too flung himself face downward. His bats—upside down—slithered into the catwalk.

Maybank had been watching those bats—the illuminated discs on which his life depended—when suddenly they vanished. In a fraction-second of indecision he couldn't think what had happened, didn't know what to do. Before he realized where he was, the Wildcat hit the deck. She hit it obliquely at eighty miles an hour, one wheel thudding on to the flight deck, the other overhanging the batting platform. Realizing, too late, what had happened, Maybank tried to swing back. But his wingtip dipped into the steel-plated deck. Instantly the Wildcat flicked on to her back. In an arc of flame she slewed across the flight deck, ploughed into the barrier, reared on to her tail, then, broken-backed, toppled into the catwalk. A sheet of white-hot flame seared

46

out of the wreckage; one of her cannon jammed at 'fire' and sprayed the island with a 20 mm. cannon shell; and a flood of blazing petrol swept half the length of the flight deck. It looked for one terrible moment as if the whole of the carrier was a sea of fire.

For perhaps three seconds *Viper* was frozen silent in horror. There was no sound except the crack of cannon fire and the hiss and roar of flames. Then the tannoy blared out: 'Emergency! Emergency!' The frightened voice jerked men into action. Out of the catwalks scrambled the fire-fighters. They rushed at the shattered aircraft, spraying it with great gouts of foam. The flames hissed and flared, weakened and died. Behind the firefighters came the asbestos-coated rescue party, with ropes and mats and acetylene torches. Two of them scrambled on to the burning fuselage. They wrenched open the cockpit-hood. They lifted Maybank out. He was unconscious, but—miraculously —still alive. As they carried him below, the shattered Wildcat was jettisoned over the side.

With the aircraft gone and the fires damped out, the flight deck seemed suddenly very dark and very quiet, with people stumbling about uncertainly and cursing softly as they tripped over arrestor wires and broken pieces of plane. It was near the island that Captain Jardine came face to face with his son. They looked at each other. Even in the pale glow of the landing lights the Captain could see on his son's face the lines of pain, the hollow, haunted eyes. He guessed what had happened. For a second his face crumpled, then he spoke very gently.

'It wasn't your fault, Ian,' he said.

Young Jardine turned away. He stumbled below. He threw himself on to his bunk. He clenched his hands; his knees he drew up to his chin. He didn't try to minimize what he had been responsible for. A lesser man would have found excuses, or shrugged the issue aside; but young Jardine faced his conscience. I killed him, he thought, as surely as if I had taken a shotgun and blown out his brains. The serpents of remorse knotted round his heart.

But it was when his thoughts shifted from Maybank to himself that his suffering really began. Then, as he thought not only of what he had done but also of why he had done it, his grief turned slowly to shame. He reminded himself that *Viper*'s other batsman had also seen an aircraft thundering towards him; the other batsman had saved the aircraft; but he, Jardine, had saved himself. There, he thought, is the difference between a brave man and a coward. His shame bit deeply; it tore at the very roots of his nature (and shame is more unendurable than sorrow, for the wounds of self-realization cut a man more keenly than the most poignant agonies of the heart). Alone that night in his cabin it seemed to young Jardine that the knowledge of what he had done would be with him for ever. But I could have borne it all, he thought, if it hadn't been for Father. There, he knew, was the root of his misery, the kernel of his shame: that his father's doubts about him had been justified: that at the moment of crisis he had taken the coward's way out.

He sat up and poured out a glass of water. His hand was trembling. What a lot of water, he thought, isn't going into the glass. He was trying to hold the glass steady when there was a knock on his cabin door. It was his steward. He brought a cup of cocoa, and the news that a Swordfish was due to be landed in twenty minutes. After he had handed Jardine the cocoa, he didn't leave, but stood awkwardly, shifting a little from foot to foot. At last he said:

'I thought you'd like to know, sir, I've just been down to Sick Bay. The M.O. thinks Lieutenant Maybank's going to be all right.'

Jardine stopped trembling.

'Thank you,' he whispered, 'for telling me that. Thank you very much.'

He looked at the man curiously. He knew nothing about him; couldn't even remember his name.

'I didn't know,' he said, 'you were Lieutenant Maybank's steward, too.'

'I'm not, sir. I just thought you'd like to know.'

Jardine was moved. The little act of kindness brought him comfort, brought a glow of warmth to the cold places of his heart. But almost at once the glow faded and died; of course, he thought, he doesn't know what really happened.

After drinking his cocoa, he went slowly up to the crewroom. He had to go there to collect his bats; but the thought of facing the other pilots and observers appalled him. They, he thought, would know.

The crewroom was lit dimly by pale blue lights, and in the half darkness and with aircrew continually moving about, he hoped to slip unobtrusively in and out. But it was not to be. The C.O. recognized him and came across the room.

'Ah, Bats!' he said. 'You've a few minutes to spare. We've kept some coffee for you.'

'I've just had some, thanks.'

'Well, come and have some more. Over here.'

They sat, facing each other, in a quiet corner of the room. Jardine didn't look up. He concentrated on stirring his coffee. The C.O. watched him.

'That was a bad crash,' he said at last.

Jardine was silent.

'I expect it's shaken you up.'

'Yes.'

'You mustn't,' the C.O. said, 'take it too hard. No batsman could have done more.'

Jardine shook his head.

'It was my fault,' he whispered.

'No, never think that. You did everything you could.'

Viper rolled awkwardly as she swung into wind, and the tannoy clicked in. 'Stand by,' came the announcement, 'to land one Swordfish.' Jardine picked up his bats.

'I'd better,' he said, 'be going.'

'And when you've finished the landing we want you for a solo four.'

'Thanks,' said Jardine. 'I'd like that.'

For the rest of the night, in between landing the Swordfish, he alternately played solo and slept. He realized

49

with a slightly hysterical relief that nobody could have seen exactly what had happened; in a carrier-landing all eyes are on the plane, and the batsman at night is invisible. So his shame would be private rather than public; a secret cross that he could bear alone. He thought at first that it would be more endurable that way. But later he was not sure. For gradually—like the poison of a secret vice—the fear that he was a coward came to obsess him; it was a fear he felt he could never escape; a secret he could never share; the tiger in his blood.

He knew too that there was one man who knew his secret: the one man he wished, above all others, to keep it from—his father.

.   .   .   .   .

As soon as the shadowing aircraft had been destroyed, Jardine reimposed radio silence. Then he altered course, taking the convoy further westward, away from the Norwegian shore. Hour after hour at top speed his ships crashed silently through heavy head seas, straining to get as far as possible from the area they had last been sighted in; for other reconnaissance aircraft, they knew, would soon take up the search.

All that night as they headed westward the weather steadily worsened; and by dawn, in spite of a reduction of speed, the vessels were shipping green water, great cataracts of foam swirling shoulder deep across their fore decks. But still the anti-submarine patrols were continued. Jardine wanted desperately—and for more reasons than one —to stop flying; but now that his convoy had been sighted the threat of U-boat attacks grew with every hour. He had no option but to keep his planes in the air.

At ten o'clock a faint lightening of the eastern sky told Jardine that behind the belts of cloud a pale anaemic sun was hoisting itself over the horizon. Sunrise was a favourite time for surprise attacks. Lookouts were doubled; gun-crews were closed up at action stations. But the half-expected U-boats and planes never came. All morning and most of the afternoon the vessels headed north-westward, undisturbed; and Jardine was beginning to think that his convoy—thanks to Maybank—had managed to escape, when, just as light was ebbing out of the sky and the mercury of the bridge thermometer was sinking below the zero mark, a Junkers reconnaissance plane swept at sea level across the convoy's bow. Ack-ack patterned the sky around her, but she escaped into cloud.

Jardine never saw the Junkers, but he heard the gun-fire, and as reports of the action were flashed back to *Viper* he became resigned to the inevitable. He knew what would happen next. He was not surprised when an hour later their radar picked up four aircraft, heading towards the convoy. By the time they heard, high above them, the throb of aircraft engines, it was quite dark.

The first plane passed directly over the convoy without sighting it. The second passed several miles astern. But the third spotted them through a rift in the cloud. She came lower; she began to circle them a little out of gun-range; she called the other aircraft back. Soon the throb of their engines filled the arctic sky, and this time Jardine knew there would be no throwing them off.

The aircraft were from Mosjoen; and throughout the night, in relays of four relieved every couple of hours, they clung to the convoy. The ships altered course and speed; their ack-ack guns cracked open the sky; but hour after hour, above the roar of the gale and the hiss and foam of ice-black waves, the monotonous beat of the shadowing aircraft circled Jardine's ships.

The protagonists had made contact. The skirmishing was over. The battle was about to begin.

And that evening Jardine became aware that his convoy would soon have yet another adversary: the weather. His ships were now passing under an occluded front, a subsidiary belt of turbulence that radiated south-eastward out of a vast depression centred off the tip of Greenland. Even under this minor front conditions were bad; with the wind gusting to forty knots, great wide-spaced rollers sweeping over the ships, and squalls of snow being driven horizontally across the sea. But the occluded front was only a forerunner of the storm centre itself. It was a storm centre of vast dimensions and terrible intensity (the wind at its centre was estimated at a hundred and fifteen miles an hour), and that night it began to reel south-eastward, straight for the advancing ships.

5

THE wind increased, the sea rose, the temperature sank to minus twenty, the aircraft circled the convoy. Hour after hour the throb of their engines vibrated among the banks of cloud.

At midnight Jardine went below. He had hoped to rest until dawn, but it seemed to him that his head had barely settled on to the pillow when the whirr of a voice-pipe jerked him out of his sleep. He picked up the speaking-tube.

'Stone here, sir.' The voice was puzzled, slightly apprehensive. 'Twenty to thirty aircraft, heading directly for us.'

'What's their range?'

'Forty miles.'

'I'll come up.'

Jardine rolled off his bunk. He pulled on his oilskins. Then he looked at his watch. The hands pointed to a little after 3 a.m. They aren't, he thought, wasting any time.

Viper was pitching violently as he clambered up to the bridge; twice he had to clutch at bulkheads to avoid being flung to the deck. On his way up he looked in at the Air Operations Room. On the radar screen a well-defined patch of light stood out clearly. This, he thought, is no false alarm. This is the real thing. He looked at Stone.

'What's their range now?'

'Thirty miles.'

He nodded, clambered on to the bridge and called for the First Lieutenant.

'Action Stations,' he said.

Hooters loud and discordant brayed into every corner of the ship, and from bunks, hammocks, benches and chairs, from mess-decks, cabins, galleys and stores, men came tumbling out, half-awake, half-asleep, rubbing the tiredness out of their eyes, struggling into life-jackets, muttering, complaining, joking and cursing, as they flooded in a confused but purposeful mêlée towards ammunition-hoists, fire-points, and gun-platforms. Almost at once reports came streaming on to the bridge: 'Gun-crews closed up . . . damage-control closed up . . . engine room closed up', and inside five minutes the carrier was at action stations.

Then, restless and slightly puzzled, Jardine paced the bridge. His convoy had been discovered, shadowed, now it was about to be attacked. But what form would the attack take? The night was dark; the sea was high with wide-spaced thirty-foot waves; the wind was a steady forty knots, gusting to over fifty in the squalls of snow. Under these conditions accurate bombing would be almost impossible; a torpedo attack would be out of the question.

The aircraft closed in. Every couple of minutes Stone relayed their bearing and range to the bridge. 'Bearing 085°, range 20. . . . Bearing 080°, range 15. . . . Bearing 073°, range 10. . . .' The planes, Jardine realized, were not heading directly for them, but were passing a shade ahead. Suddenly he smiled; for the planes' direction had given him the clue he needed; he knew now what he had to face. He waited until the aircraft were very near, until the beat of their engines filled the sky; then he turned quickly to the Yeoman.

'Signal the convoy "Emergency turn, 90° to port".'

The Aldis lights winked out.

As though jerked by the same invisible string, cruisers, merchantmen, destroyers and corvettes put over their helms. They spun round, almost on their axes; and as they turned they came beam on to the heavy seas. They rolled wickedly. The corvettes and smaller merchantmen dipped scuppers under and rose quivering, with ice-green cataracts streaming off their upper decks, but of all the ships none rolled as wickedly as *Viper*; for, as she turned, the carrier fell into a trough; the great seas came crashing into her beam; men were flung to the deck; a lashing in the hangar parted, and the tail of a Swordfish broke loose and splintered itself to shreds; it seemed an eternity before the carrier rolled back, with a terrible vibrating shudder, on to an even keel. The convoy had barely straightened on to its new course when the cloud to starboard burst into a ruddy glow, and three parachute flares, storm-tossed and burning fiercely, came swinging out of the night. And behind the flares dropped the mines, drifting by parachute into an empty sea. The minebelt that would—but for Jardine's turn— have been laid across the convoy's bow now fell harmlessly along its flank. Along the edge of darkness the ships moved quietly forward.

The flares spluttered and died; the throb of aircraft weakened and faded; the tension relaxed. The danger, many thought, was over.

Jardine was glad to have Stone's report that the aircraft were heading back for Norway. He was glad to have one or two senior officers congratulate him on having avoided the mines so neatly. But in his mind was a core of doubt, a fragment of disbelief. It seemed strange that the attack should have been avoided so easily. In fact, he thought, it's more than strange; it's unbelievable. He kept his fears to himself—but he also kept *Viper* at action stations.

And it was not long before his fears were justified.

The first hint of further trouble was a message from the patrolling Swordfish; her observer reported they were investigating a contact dead ahead at a range of fifteen miles.

'Dead ahead,' the First Lieutenant grunted. 'Quite a coincidence.'

Jardine nodded.

Frightening in its unexpectedness, the thud of depth-charges echoed out of the darkness, and a few seconds later the Yeoman of Signals handed Jardine an 'in contact' report from a corvette of the advanced screen. And almost at the same moment the Swordfish radioed again, reporting another U-boat contact, fine on their port bow. Jardine felt a stab of fear. So, he thought, you aren't so clever after all. You've turned the convoy straight into a pack of U-boats.

He stood irresolute, hands clasping the bridge rail. His convoy was poised on the edge of disaster now. Already he had made one mistake. Another would be fatal. Possible courses of action passed through his mind. To the west were U-boats; to the north were mines; if he turned south, he would expose the convoy's flank; if he turned east, he would hamstring his most effective weapon of defence—his air-craft—for every time he wanted to fly them off or land them on, he would have to turn *Viper* on the opposite course to the convoy. An idea, as yet vague and half formed, began to take shape. He lifted the flap of a voice-pipe.

'Met.'

'Sir?'

'Captain here. Give me the surface wind. Quickly.'

There was a pause, a rustling of papers, then: '280°, sir. 30 knots, gusting 45 to 50.'

He snapped the voice-pipe down.

'Our best chance,' he said, 'is to go slap through the middle of 'em.'

.   .   .   .   .

Young Jardine stirred in his sleep. He heard the subdued hum of conversation, the shifting of tables and chairs, and the scuffling of feet. He opened a reluctant eye and saw that the crewroom was full. He caught a glimpse of his father, walking out of the room; he must, he realized, have just finished talking to the squadron. He swung his legs over the side of his bunk.

'What's happening?' he asked.

'We've run into a pack of U-boats,' Marsden told him. 'The Swordfish are taking off to keep them down.'

Young Jardine said nothing. He knew what would

happen in the next few hours: with aircraft constantly taking-off and landing-on, he would be kept on deck; he would be batting almost continually; he would get no sleep. Yet he needed sleep desperately now, craved for it as a man in pain craves for morphia. The C.O. looked at him: saw the white face, with the little beads of sweat fringing the temples, and the tired, dark-ringed eyes. If he cracks now, he thought, the convoy's lost. He wondered if the Captain realized how much responsibility he was passing on to his son.

'Why not,' he said, 'go to the Ops Room? It's quieter there. You can get your head down till you're called.'

'I'll do that,' Jardine said.

The Operations Room was quieter than the crewroom, quieter and far less crowded. Before Jardine bedded down he took a look at the U-boat plot. There were, he noticed, already seven U-boats close to the convoy. The position of each was marked on the plot by a black cross; the crosses were strung out in a shallow crescent ahead of the advancing ships; and some of them were very near. As he was settling down to sleep, Stone came across to the plot. In his hand were two more crosses.

'Looks like being quite a night,' he said.

A roaring crescendo from the flight deck, just above their heads, told them the first of the Swordfish was taking off. And I hope, Jardine thought, you stay airborne a nice long time. Then I can get some sleep.

But in less than half an hour he felt Stone shaking him by the shoulder. The Air Operations Officer, he noticed, was looking less imperturbable than usual; and a glance at the U-boat plot told him why. There were seventeen crosses now, and they were very close.

He struggled into his oilskins and clambered on to the flight deck. It might, he knew, be a long time before he returned below. Yet, now the landing-on was about to begin, his tiredness receded a little and he felt a stir of exhilaration, a glow of response to the challenge that lay ahead. Here, he told himself as he stumbled over the flattened arrestor wires, lay his chance of atonement, his hope of expiation: in spite of darkness and snow, in spite of wind and sea, in spite of any and every adverse circumstance he was determined—somehow—to get every plane safely down.

In the few minutes before the first Swordfish returned, he gathered from the Deck Officer a confused impression of what had happened in the last half-hour.

The convoy, it seemed, had swung a few degrees to port. They were heading straight for the U-boats now; straight too into the forty-knot wind.

Young Jardine was quick to see the advantage of this; *Viper* could now fly-off and land her aircraft without altering course, without moving out of station. Already eleven Swordfish were in the air, blanketing the U-boats, keeping them down, preventing their surfacing to launch their torpedoes. But the planes, the Deck Officer told him, were having a difficult job; the U-boats were many and determined, the weather was appalling, he doubted if they could keep their offensive up. Jardine guessed what lay at the root of his doubt: the fear that many of the Swordfish would be bound to crash on landing. The Deck Officer's doubt was like a whetstone to the edge of his resolve.

A message came through from the bridge that the first plane was approaching the carrier. He walked across to the batting platform. Soon he could see the pale blue navigation lights drifting towards him. He held his bats level.

The approach was not a good one. The Swordfish came in crabwise and too fast. Jardine waved her off. I don't care, he thought, how tired you are. I don't care how many attempts you have to make. You'll have to do better than that. The engine roar deepened as the Swordfish rose, in a flurry of snow, away from the flight deck. She vanished into the night; it was several minutes before her lights appeared again, drifting towards the carrier's stern.

The second approach was no better than the first; again the aircraft came in crabwise and fast; and again Jardine waved her off. As she rose awkwardly away from the deck, a message came through for Jardine on the ship's telephone. He leant over the edge of his batting platform and picked up the receiver. He was connected through to Commander Flying.

'That you, Bats?'

'Yes, sir.'

'What's wrong?'

'She's coming in too fast.'

He heard a mutter of conversation from the other end of the line; then a voice, which he recognized as his father's, said, 'I'll speak to him.'

'Are you there, Bats?'

'Yes, sir.'

'We think the Swordfish is damaged. You'll have to get her down as best you can.'

Young Jardine began to tremble. So much, he thought, for my hope of bringing them all in safely; the very first one's going to crash. He moistened his lips. His mouth juddered against the mouthpiece of the telephone.

'Der-der-der-do you know how bad the damage is?'

'No. Her radio's out of action.'

'Could you pur-pur-put a searchlight on her?'

'We've thought of that. I daren't risk it. Not with U-boats about.'

There was a pause, then the Captain said: 'I'm sorry, Ian. You'll have to do the best you can. Good luck.'

He heard the click as his father put down the receiver. He looked at *Viper*'s round-down and saw it rising and falling in great uneven pulsations. He looked into the night and a flurry of snow plastered across his eyes. What chance have I got, he thought, of landing a plane that's damaged on a night like this?

. . . . .

Summers and James had been standing-by when the early U-boat reports came through; so they were the first crew to get away. They collected their parachutes, scrambled down the flight deck and clambered into the Swordfish

59

parked on the carrier's stern. Summers could tell at once that things weren't going to be easy. As he was warming the aircraft up, a chock slid from under one of his wheels, and the plane slithered across the ice-coated deck; it took two dozen ratings of the flight-deck handling party to haul her back into position against the blustering wind.

The take-off itself he did on instruments, for it was too dark to see the horizon.

As soon as the plane left the deck the wind snatched at her, flinging her almost against the island. Summers had to fight desperately to keep her under control. He was appalled at the way the aircraft bucketed about, as though an unseen giant were tossing her capriciously from hand to hand. Great hammer-blows of wind battered her with insensate malevolence. His instruments went mad; the artificial horizon tilting crazily, the compass swinging like a pendulum and the altimeter rocketing up and down; and all the while there poured into the open cockpits the plastering snow and the terrible aching cold. He didn't fly the plane, he fought her; fought her with the singleness of purpose of a cow-puncher riding an untamed stallion. Grimly he forced her up to three hundred feet; then he held her on a westerly course, a course that took them over the advanced screen, towards the U-boats.

And how many U-boats there were!

On the screen of his A.S.V.X. James could see the pear-shaped shadows lying in a semi-circle ahead of the advancing ships; there were at least a dozen of them.

At their briefing Stone had given each plane a sector to patrol, so many square miles to keep free of U-boats. Their sector lay almost dead ahead. As far as James could see there was only one U-boat in it, about nine miles ahead of the convoy. He called through a course that took them directly towards it (there was no time for refinements such as attacking down-wind, and their job in any case was not so much to sink the U-boats as to put them down; and keep them down). When they got to within four miles of the U-boat, Summers took the Swordfish down to a hundred and fifty feet. He checked his depth-charges and his star-shell release gear. He had been flying anti-submarine aircraft for over a year now. So far he had never even seen a U-boat, let alone sunk one. Tonight, he thought, my luck will change.

But he was wrong.

With the range down to a mile and a half, the shadow on James's screen began to fade. The U-boat had picked them up. She was crash-diving fast. By the time Summers's star-shell lit the sea where she had been the U-boat had vanished. They circled the area for several minutes, but she didn't reappear.

'I expect,' said James, 'there'll be others.'

He was right. There were many others.

In the confusion of the next twenty minutes too many U-boats surfaced in their sector for them to attack them all. But they homed on two: the two nearest the convoy. The first dived while they were still a good way short. The second, braver or less vigilant, stayed on the surface until they were almost on top of her. Then at the last minute she too started to submerge. In the light of his starshell Summers thought he could see her slick—the little circle of churned-up sea marking the spot where she had dived. He flung the Swordfish seaward. But the closer he got to the slick, the less certain he became. Was it the vortex of a dive, or was it simply a patch of wind-whitened sea? At the last second he decided it was worth taking a chance; he pressed his release button, and four depth-charges, straddling the slick, scythed into the sea.

He banked away as the tall columns of water heaved skyward. Then he returned, and another salvo of starshell yellowed the sea. But they saw no wreckage; no heartening patch of oil. For five minutes they circled the area, hope-fully dropping starshell and flares. But of the U-boat—if indeed there had ever been one—they saw no sign. Dis-appointed, their depth-charges gone, they set course for the carrier.

And almost at once, fine on their starboard bow, at a

range of only three miles, another U-boat broke surface.

But all their depth-charges had gone; they had nothing left with which to attack it.

Their job, Summers knew, was to put the U-boats down. This, he argued with his observer, they could do without depth-charges. They had only to home on this latest target, and it, like the others, would dive for safety. Rather against his better judgment James agreed that the idea was worth a try.

Flying downwind they were almost on top of the U-boat before they realized what was happening, realized that this time their target wasn't crash-diving but was staying to fight. Summers held course as long as he dared, hoping to force the U-boat down; but she remained obstinately on the surface. He was very close to her before he banked the plane aside (with his depth-charges gone there was no point in flying right over the top of her). As he turned, a sudden burst of flak cracked open the sky. He thought at first that the innocent-looking bars of light were passing well beneath them. But suddenly either the U-boat rolled, deflecting her fire, or else her gunner saw the shadow of the plane; for a long burst of tracer came slashing straight for Summers's eyes. He flung the plane aside. But too late. With a splintering crash and a smell of burning cordite, the tracer tore into the Swordfish. A spate of bullets shattered her starboard landing-wheel, sliced through her wing fabric, then rose diagonally through the pilot's cockpit. They seared past Summers's face, then splattered into the instrument panel, showering the cockpit with broken glass. Summers was blinded. A sudden surge of pain wrenched at his left foot. What a stupid, unnecessary way, he thought, to get yourself shot down. Trying to pull the plane level, he kicked at the port rudder-bar. He almost fainted in agony. Looking down he saw that his left foot was a mass of bleeding pulp—the tracer had sliced off his toes and shredded away the sole of his foot. The flak was all around them now, beating into the aircraft like some terrible cosmic hail; but as the plane toppled seaward, it started to pass over the top of them, then it died away. Summers centralized the control-column. To his surprise the Swordfish levelled off. He heard his observer calling him, as if from far away. For several seconds he was too sick, too dazed, to know where the voice was coming from; then he realized that James was shouting through his gosport-tubes—the emergency voice-pipe. So their radio was out of action.

'Ted! Ted!' The voice came to him muffled and hollow. 'Are you all right?'

'Yes,' he said, 'I'm all right.'

He looked at his foot. He felt curiously little pain—as long as he didn't touch the rudder-bar. But he felt sick: sick and dazed and weak. He wondered how much blood he was losing. He wondered if he could get back to the carrier before he fainted.

The next ten minutes seemed endless as eternity: a timeless purgatory of disappointment and difficulty and pain. If it hadn't been for James he would have given up, given up thankfully and shut his eyes and fallen asleep and let the plane slide into the sea; the longed-for sea that would have ended all his sickness and bewilderment and pain. But James's voice, insistent and matter-of-fact, kept him alive.

'Ted! Can you steer a course?'

Summers looked at his shattered instruments.

'No,' he said. 'No compass.'

'Mine's still O.K. Turn to port. I'll tell you when to level up.'

I'm damned, Summers thought, if I'll turn to port. If I touch the port rudder I'll faint. He banked the Swordfish into a turn to starboard. After James had told him to ease out of the turn, he found he could keep the plane reasonably straight by using his artificial horizon, which alone of all his instruments seemed to be undamaged.

And so, painfully and with frequent corrections of course, they headed back for the carrier. After a while a not unpleasant drowsiness began to take hold of Summers; but again his observer's voice cut through his haze of semi-consciousness:

'What height are we, Ted?'

'I don't know.'

'I think we're too high. We're above cloud.'

Summers was in no mood to argue. He pushed the stick forward; the nose of the Swordfish dropped; his speed built up; he heard the wind sighing through his struts. I hope, he thought, we go straight into the sea. But when James told him to level off he automatically obeyed.

And a few minutes later they found the convoy.

Beneath his wingtip Summers saw the dark ill-defined shadow of the ships, each with its white fleck of bow-wave. He felt a flood of thankfulness, tinged with disbelief. So they had made it after all. Now he need only do one thing more—persuade James to use his parachute—then he could shut his eyes and let the waves of pain engulf him utterly. He heard his observer calling him again.

'Ted! *Viper*'s on our port beam. Did you see her Aldis?'

'I saw it.'

'Let's be going then.'

Summers was silent. After a long time his observer asked him what was the matter. He tried desperately to fight clear of the waves of faintness that were coming now with increasing frequency. He wanted James to bale out; for he knew their chances of making a safe landing were so slender as to be almost nil. But how to persuade him? Any attempt at subtlety was more than he felt capable of, so he simply said:

'We're too badly damaged to land. You'll have to bale out.'

It was James who was silent now. Not 'we'll bale out', he thought, but 'you'll bale out'. He realized his pilot was wounded; realized he was offering him a chance to save himself. But I can't leave him now, he thought. By himself he wouldn't stand a chance. He'd give up too easily.

'Don't talk nonsense,' he said. 'Of course we can land.'

Summers could have wept.

'Please, Kit,' he said. 'Don't be a fool. You'll be all right if you bale out. Let's not both be killed.'

64

'Nobody's going to be killed. Pull yourself together.'

Summers felt too weak to argue. He asked James to signal *Viper* by Aldis to tell her they were damaged; and when his observer told him their Aldis was shattered and they had no way of contacting the carrier, he felt no emotion whatsoever.

'We'll just have to go straight in,' he said.

And James agreed.

When they were waved off the first time Summers felt angry and frustrated. He wanted to get things over—one way or another—as quickly as possible. When they were waved off the second time he felt close to tears with weakness and frustration and rage.

But James didn't let him give up.

'Have one more try,' he said.

.   .   .   .   .

For the third time Jardine picked up his bats. He knew that no one would blame him if the Swordfish crashed; but that meant nothing. He would always wonder in his own mind if there was something else he could have done, always wonder if some other signal might have saved her. He keyed himself up, determined this third time to make a supreme effort to get her down.

He thought things out. Now he knew the plane was damaged he had something concrete to work on. Twice she had come in fast. That would mean either the plane was structurally damaged and her stalling speed increased, or else that the pilot had no air-speed indicator. The latter he decided was more likely; so he'd take the risk of slowing her down. Twice she had come in crabwise. That would mean her rudder was damaged; this was something beyond his control, beyond the pilot's control too; so crabwise he would have to land her.

The deck had been cleared. The tannoy had blared 'Emergency landing' and the fire-fighters had come scrambling into the catwalk. Silence fell over the carrier as the plane began her third approach.

It was a long, straight approach; an approach which gave batsman and pilot plenty of time to get on terms; and it was a better approach than the previous ones. Jardine realized he wasn't the only one making a superhuman effort. Poor devil, he thought, you're still coming in too fast; he moved one of his bats out of sight. And this time his signal was obeyed. The plane slowed; her tail dropped, and her 'attitude' light swung into Jardine's line of vision. He held his bats level. Once he signalled the plane to drop a little lower, once to come a little more slowly; otherwise he let the pilot land himself. Soon the plane was very near, poised half-stalling high over the round-down. *Viper*'s stern swung obligingly up. Now, thought Jardine, for God's sake do as I tell you. High as she was he gave her the signal to cut, and in the same second signalled up her port wing. The roar of the engine died; the wingtip tilted level, and the plane came crashing down flush on the second arrestor wire. She hit the flight deck heavily: heavily but squarely. Her undercarriage snapped off, and she squelched on to the deck plates like an over-ripe plum falling on to crazy-paving. Bits of her shattered landing gear shot across the deck, her lower wings splintered, her back broke, and she lay smashed but mercifully still in a widening pool of petrol.

The second after she hit the deck James was tumbling out of his cockpit. But Summers did not move. The ratings who scrambled up the side of the fuselage found him slumped over his stick. His eyes were open but unseeing, his face was dead white, and at the bottom of the cockpit was a slowly widening pool of blood.

'Jesus!' one of the ratings whispered. 'He's dead.'

But when with the help of a doctor they hauled him out of the cockpit, they found he was not dead but had fainted—fainted at the very moment his plane had hit the deck.

.   .   .   .   .

In the hour after the U-boats were sighted sixteen patrols were flown. Their pattern, except in the way they ended, was much the same as Summers's. Time and again the Swordfish picked up a U-boat on their A.S.V.X. Time and again they homed on to their target to within a couple of miles. And time and again they found that the U-boat got wind of them and dived. Not for these planes the spectacular night attack, with rockets, flares and starshells lighting up the midnight sea; only the everlasting casting around and the tantalizing unrewarding search. It was exhausting, unspectacular work; but it was because of patrols like these that the convoy began early that morning to bludgeon its way through the encircling pack.

Victory did not come easily; every mile was bitterly contested, and for a couple of hours the issue hung in the balance; but in the end the night belonged to *Viper*'s Swordfish.

Most of the aircraft Stone concentrated dead ahead; so that the U-boats in front of the convoy found themselves unable to surface, unable to get a bearing on their target. Gradually they were forced aside, pushed outward on to either flank. And here they were pounced on, and pushed further outward, by the destroyers and corvettes.

But it was one thing for a carrier to launch such an air offensive, and quite another for her to maintain it hour after hour. The strain on the pilots and observers was unbelievable. And an equally heavy strain was imposed on the ratings in flight deck and hangar. For a single hold up, and Jardine's counter-offensive would have ground to a standstill; the convoy would have been left defenceless.

But there was no hold up. That night the squadron ratings worked as they had never worked before. The instant each plane touched down, they came swarming across the ice-coated deck; they held it steady against the tug of wind and tilt of deck; they disconnected its arrestor hook; they folded its wings; they manhandled it aft; they lashed it on to the lift. The hydraulics hummed and sighed; the lift sank; the aircraft vanished into the darkness between the decks. Seconds later it was unlashed and trundled into the bedlam of the brightly lit hangar. Here all was warmth and colour; here, under the garish arc lamps in an atmosphere redolent with varnish, fabric, and petrol, each aircraft was serviced, tested, re-armed, re-fuelled, and rushed back to the flight deck. Its engine was started up. Its pilot and observer came tumbling into the cockpits, and within twenty minutes of landing the plane was again in the air.

And thanks to the speed and efficiency of the turn-round, the air offensive was sustained, hour after hour.

But the work in flight deck and hangar would have been of no account if the planes had not, in the first place, landed safely. That they did so was due to young Jardine's batting.

In the first hour he landed thirteen planes, in the second hour sixteen, in the third hour the Swordfish came thudding down so frequently that he lost count. But the numbers did not matter. What did matter was that he landed all of them safely.

For the rest of that night he never left the batting platform. Before each landing began he keyed himself up to a tension close to breaking point. He sharpened his perception to a razor-edge of awareness. He watched each plane as it thundered toward him with the intentness of a hunter taking his final shot at a charging elephant. No flicker of a wingtip escaped his notice; he found a meaning for every change in the beat of an engine. He came to recognize each pilot by the style of his landing. Some, he found, liked landing off a turn; some off a straight run-in. Some had certain weaknesses; these he anticipated and allowed for. Some had a flair for doing certain types of landing especially well; these he remembered and made use of. He stood there hour after hour controlling the approaching planes until his eyes were raw with watering, and his arms ached with the weight of his bats, and his legs felt anchored to the deck by leaden weights. After the first hour he began to shiver, in sudden unexpected spasms; for the flight deck was bitterly cold. Yet its coldness was not as chilling as the fear which, each time a plane came in to land, closed round his heart. Would this, he wondered, be

68

the one to crash? It seemed impossible that in the darkness and driving snow, in the clawing wind and tempestuous sea, plane after plane should touch down safely. Sooner or later, he felt sure, he would signal wrongly, or too slowly and another plane—like Maybank's—would shatter itself on the iron deck. It was the fear of this that gave him the strength to go on, that kept him keyed up long after the normal breaking-point of physical and mental strain had passed. That, and the thought of his father.

Several people did what they could to help; but their help could not amount to much. The Flight Deck Officer saw that he was brought hot cocoa; the M.O. helped him to change his gloves and flying-boots and kept him supplied with heat-giving kapok pads; a few of the pilots came to have a word with him—but they could not stay for long—and at the end of the third hour his father sent a message of congratulation from the bridge. That pleased him; made him feel that his expiation was under way; strengthened his resolve not to relax.

Men who are highly strung can sometimes rise to an emergency in a way that is quite out of character. That night Jardine proved he was such a man. The strength of Atlas and the red badge of courage were—for the moment—his. And in them he rejoiced. They may, he thought, be like the harlequin costume worn at a midnight ball, borrowed accoutrements; on loan; strictly returnable at dawn. That doesn't matter. For the moment they're mine.

And while young Jardine was fighting his own personal battle on *Viper*'s flight deck, in the surrounding sea a greater battle by far swelled to its climax: the clash between U-boats and Swordfish.

The U-boats were in difficulty. The fact that the convoy hadn't turned but was heading straight towards them disrupted their plans. Conditions for launching their torpedoes were appalling. Out of the darkness, the tumbling mountain-sides of water came crashing into them; within a few minutes of surfacing they became sheathed in a veneer of ice; the wind plucked men off their decks and smothered them to lifelessness in torrents of driven spume; and every time they surfaced, within a few minutes (sometimes a few seconds) they heard the hated throb of a Swordfish heading directly for them. They had only two alternatives: stay under and miss their chance of launching an attack, or stay on the surface and fight.

Some tried to compromise; tried to work their way in little dashes, surfacing for bearings in between, round to the convoy's flank. There, they hoped, the aircraft would be less active. They were right. But the depth-charges of Jardine's destroyers and corvettes were as effective as those of his Swordfish; and in the end these compromisers too were faced with the same alternative: fight or run.

Most of them stayed to fight.

Some fought with anger, some with despair, and some with cunning and skill. But the result was generally the same; they were either crippled or pushed aside or sunk.

The first U-boat to be sunk fought with anger. Her captain lay obstinately on the surface, his ack-ack manned. The first Swordfish to attack her met with a hot reception and retired with a shredded wingtip. The second Swordfish crippled her with a stick of depth-charges dropped, under heavy fire, a little too far astern to send her to the bottom. By the time the third Swordfish found her, she was very close to the convoy; but her crew were exhausted; her fire was ragged; and the Swordfish was able to pattern her with a precisely placed stick of depth-charges that literally blew her in half.

The second U-boat to be sunk fought with despair. Her captain estimated the convoy's course and speed, dived beneath the patrolling planes, then tried to surface a little ahead of the advancing ships. But as the U-boat started to rise, he heard, bearing down on him, the engine beat of an attacking warship. He tried to dive deeper; but the corvette had him in firm Asdic contact. Two patterns of depth-charges blew his U-boat to the surface; a third broke her back and sent her, twisting and disintegrating, to the bed of the sea.

Of the others, one was sunk by a Swordfish and one by a destroyer; and five were so badly damaged that they could only limp painfully aside.

So it was that by the end of the third hour the convoy had broken through; and out of the eighteen submarines that had lain in wait for Jardine's ships, over half were left sunk or shattered in the convoy's wake.

But the price of victory was high.

Towards the end of the second hour two U-boats managed to avoid both planes and warships, managed to break through the protecting screen and launch their torpedoes.

In each case their attack was carried out quickly, under pressure, and at extreme range. In the heavy seas the torpedoes ran erratically; some sank, some ran wide. Only one found its target. But that, for some hundred and twenty men, was one too many. A corvette on the convoy's flank was hit squarely, about twenty feet from her bow. She was hit while running at high speed, and at such a spot and angle that the blast of burning air from the explosion swept straight into her ammunition locker. Before the roar of the initial explosion had died, another and more terrible sound rang out: a single long-drawn boo-oo-oo-oom that echoed in hollow diminuendo among the banks of cloud. A destroyer, disregarding its own safety and Jardine's orders, switched on a searchlight. The swathe of whiteness cut across the sea where the corvette had been. The sea was empty. The searchlight moved from side to side; then reluctantly, as if unwilling to believe what it saw, it came to rest on a falling mushroom of dust, a brownish haze of burnt air and falling fragments, all that remained of what had once been a corvette.

Jardine's escort was small. The loss of even a single warship meant a serious weakening of his defences. But the sinking of the corvette was not the most crippling blow he had to face that night.

For from their battle with the U-boats two of his Swordfish failed to return.

One mistimed her take-off. She staggered with agonizing slowness off the end of the flight deck, then fell stalling on to the crest of a wave. The instant she touched the water she cartwheeled on to her back and sank. The other Swordfish was shot down by a U-boat's ack-ack. Neither crew was saved.

At the start of the convoy there had been fifteen Swordfish in *Viper*'s hangar. Now there were only eleven. Jardine realized that his anti-submarine defences were being whittled gradually away.

And a little before dawn, in the moment of victory, *Viper* suffered yet another loss. A Swordfish crashed on landing.

It was what young Jardine had been dreading for the last four hours. So far plane after plane had thudded safely down (in close on fifty landings the only mishaps had been a single broken oleo leg, and one plane rolling gently into the barrier). But it was too much to expect that the miracle should be self-perpetuating, that each safe touch-down should be followed by another; and early in the fifth hour a plane went over the side.

Was it, young Jardine later asked himself, the approach of dawn, the almost imperceptible lightening of the sky, that made him unconsciously relax? Did his concentration falter because he knew the patrols were being recalled and his ordeal was drawing to an end? Was it a 'pilot's error'—those words so easy to write afterwards on the accident report sheet? Or was the error his? It was something he could never be sure of: a doubt that would never be wholly dispelled.

The Swordfish came in to land at a moment when the wind seemed to have steadied. She made a long, straight, perfectly normal approach, a better approach than many of the other planes had managed. But as she hung poised for landing, *Viper* pitched suddenly forward. Her stern was flung violently up. Before he could wave the Swordfish away, the round-down smashed into her; her undercarriage was snapped off, and with a shriek of lacerated metal she slewed screaming across the deck. Her hook missed the arrestor wires by only a couple of inches—but the inches might as well have been miles. For with a splintering crash the plane fell into the catwalk, tore through carley-floats, bofors and oerlikons, hung for a moment suspended by the folds of a grappling net, then toppled broken-backed into the sea.

Young Jardine covered his eyes. His bats fell to the deck. He took one step across his batting platform; then the whole carrier began to undulate, like water flowing over a scenic railway. His knees buckled, and he crashed unconscious to the deck.

'Emergency! Emergency!' blared the tannoy. 'Aircraft over the starboard side.'

There was a rush of feet across the flight deck. Carley floats and lifebelts were flung into the sea. Men crowded the rails. But in the half-darkness they could see only a formless shadow, as slowly the broken plane drifted past *Viper*'s stern. Of the crew there was no sign.

A searchlight flickered over the wreckage. Instantly Captain Jardine's voice came clearly over the tannoy.

'Put out that light.'

The beam faded. A rating swore softly. And into the darkness the wreckage drifted away.

The Flight Deck Officer picked young Jardine up. He pushed the lip of a brandy flask into his mouth. Most of the liquid ran perversely over Jardine's teeth and trickled down his neck, but a little found its way into his throat. He spluttered and sat up. He looked around him, shivered once and then lay still.

'Hey, Bats!' The Flight Deck Officer was alarmed. 'Are you O.K.?'

'Yes, I'm fine. I feel absolutely wonderful.'

He stood up, picked his bats off the deck and climbed uncertainly on to the batting platform. The Flight Deck Officer clambered up beside him.

'Sit down,' he said. 'You don't look so good.'

Slowly Jardine turned round. His face was grey; his skin was stretched taut; his forehead was beaded with sweat.

73

'Leave me alone,' he whispered.

As the Flight Deck Officer stood awkwardly, uncertain what to do, a messenger came hurrying down the deck. He handed young Jardine a signal pad.

'Message from the Cap'n, sir,' he said.

Jardine pushed the signal away.

'I know,' he said, 'he doesn't have to tell me what to do. Signal the next plane in.'

That, he thought, was supposed to be the answer, wasn't it? You fell off your fairy-cycle; your father told you to pick yourself up and try again. You crashed your motor-bike; your father told you to go straight off on another. It had something to do, your father said, with not losing your nerve.

The next Swordfish, as though in answer to his prayer, made an almost perfect landing. His trembling became less violent. Somewhere, deep within him, his confidence was gradually reborn. He landed two more aircraft safely. He began to think that perhaps after all the crash had been unavoidable: hadn't been his fault.

Soon, as the U-boats dropped farther astern, more and more Swordfish were recalled, and the intervals between the landings increased. At last only two planes were left in the air, and neither was due back for over an hour.

Young Jardine realized then that he could leave his batting platform.

Quite suddenly, relief that his ordeal was over submerged every other feeling. The tension of the last six hours ebbed out of him. He sat down on the edge of his platform. The M.O. had been watching him carefully for the last couple of hours. Now he came hurrying across the deck. But before he reached him, young Jardine was asleep.

.   .   .   .   .

A little before dawn the convoy altered course, back to the northward. The U-boats had dropped well astern; they made little effort to follow. Battered and hunted to exhaustion, they had had enough.

After the turmoil of the last few hours the carrier seemed to Captain Jardine strangely silent, as she headed northward beneath a slowly paling sky. Gone was the hissing groan of the barrier as the hydraulics raised and lowered it, in time with the take-off and landing of the planes. Gone too was the grate and sigh of the lift as it rose and fell between flight deck and hangar. The planes were below, the crews were asleep. By dawn the only sounds on the flight deck were the dull roar of the wind, and the shuddering thud of *Viper*'s hull as she rose and fell among the wide-spaced waves.

But the carrier remained at action stations; and Captain Jardine remained on the bridge. He stayed there hour after hour, leaning against the starboard bridge rail. His thoughts were not of the past but of the future. He allowed himself no post-mortems on their engagement with the U-boats; that was over and done with; they had won through; 'Let the dead Past bury its dead.' His concern was with the future. Now it was light, his binoculars swept the line of the eastern horizon, where a bare mile from the carrier the torn ribbons of cloud merged into a wind-whipped sea. He tilted his binoculars up; they swept the sky, the innocent, treacherous sky. He wondered for how long it would be empty; how long it would be before the bombers found them.

6

ALL morning the convoy headed north under a ragged sky. By noon the wind was a full gale; the waves, three-quarters of a mile apart, were flooding out of the west like snow-plumed mountains; and the ships were trembling: scraps of paper caught in a wind-scoured tunnel.

And still no bombers came. Another couple of hours, thought Jardine, and the light will begin to fade. He wondered what was holding them back: perhaps the weather? He looked at the driving curtains of snow, then at the met. report that Ian MacLeod had brought him at noon. He could not remember having ever seen a more depressing forecast. He held it up to the light of a bridge lamp.

An intense depression, he read, *centred off the tip of Greenland is moving rapidly east. Very strong westerly gale will continue throughout the day, with low cloud and intermittent snow. Wind increasing and backing slowly in the evening.*

Grade 'C' forecast till 2200/8:

WIND	W.–N.W'ly 50 knots, gusting to 70 knots: increasing.
WEATHER	Cloudy with intermittent blizzards of snow.
CLOUD	9/10–10/10 at 1000 feet, with patches at sea level.
VISIBILITY	1½–2 miles: decreasing.
SEA	Very rough.
OUTLOOK FOR TONIGHT	W'ly gale persisting, backing and increasing.

He knew MacLeod, the Meteorological Officer, well; knew him for an exact, level-headed man, not given to over-statement. He called him up and told him he was coming below to see the weather chart.

.   .   .   .   .

The Meteorological Office was an almost perfect cube; eight foot long, wide and high. Along one wall lay the black bulk of the teleprinter, into which weather reports from every available source were fed by radio and coded into teleprinted sheets. On the opposite wall hung a large-scale weather chart of the north-eastern Atlantic; on it Jardine could see, even from the doorway, the isobaric circles of the vast depression.

It was, MacLeod explained, a storm-centre of staggering intensity. It had built up slowly, off the southern tip of Greenland. Then about twelve hours ago it had started to move eastward, gathering up and engulfing into its vast structure a scattering of minor depressions that lay in its path. Now at its centre the barometer was down to 27.78″; the wind had risen to a hundred and twenty miles an hour; and the whole mass, whirling like an unstable top, was reeling with gathering momentum across the convoy's path.

Jardine looked at MacLeod.

'What,' he asked, 'would happen to a ship in the middle of that?'

The Met Officer shook his head.

'That,' he said, 'Aa wouldna like tae say.'

An alarm klaxon sounded on the bridge, and there came faintly and from far away the muffled thud of gunfire. Jardine flung himself out of the room.

'Send me a wind report,' he shouted, as he scrambled up the companionway. 'Every half-hour.'

On deck the gale seemed to have increased in the few minutes he had been below. The snow had stopped now, and the cloud had risen a little, but the wind was thundering out of the west with mounting fury; it brought tears to

77

his eyes and tore the breath from his mouth. He heard again the distant roll of gunfire and saw, fine on their starboard bow, torn ribbons of ack-ack streaming above a destroyer of the advanced screen. And at the same time he spotted the plane—a solitary Junkers 88—low on the northern horizon.

Two fighter pilots, bowed low against the wind, were stumbling across the flight deck, making for the Wildcats lashed down on the carrier's stern. Jardine's first impulse was to let them take off. Then he stopped to think. Why, he asked himself, had there been only the single Junkers; and why had it fled so precipitately, with barely the pretence of an attack? He delayed his order for the fighters to leave the deck.

Twice again within the next few minutes a single Junkers approached the convoy; and twice again it veered sharply away at the first burst of gunfire. Jardine felt certain then that the attacks were feints, attempts to draw his fighters into the air, away from the convoy.

He kept the Wildcats on deck. The minutes passed.

After a while the bridge telephone tinkled, and a message came through from Stone. 'Radar contact. Twenty to twenty-five aircraft. Sea level. Bearing 095°. Range 15 miles.' It was the message he had been waiting for since dawn; the intimation that the second attack on his convoy was under way.

Twelve hours earlier a dozen Swordfish had stood between the convoy and the U-boats. Against this new attack from the air Jardine's defences were even more tenuous: seven Wildcat fighters, and the ack-ack guns of his warships and merchantmen. We'll be lucky, he thought, if we get through this with the loss of only one corvette.

He swung *Viper* into wind, and the first two Wildcats took off; they circled the convoy, gaining height, then headed east to intercept the approaching planes. Before they were out of sight the bridge telephone rang again. It was Stone with another radar report: from the opposite side of the convoy a second formation of aircraft was closing in. Another pair of Wildcats had just been brought on deck, and soon they too were airborne and climbing away from the convoy. And before the last three fighters could be wheeled on to the lift the telephone rang for the third time. The First Lieutenant's hand was trembling as he passed Jardine yet another radar report: 'Twenty-five to thirty aircraft. Sea level. Dead ahead. Range thirty miles.'

The convoy was surrounded; from three directions some seventy aircraft were closing in.

The last of *Viper*'s Wildcats tore hurtling down the flight deck. All seven planes were airborne now. The fate of the convoy was in their hands.

Gordon Blake, the pilot of the first Wildcat to take off, was a New Zealander, a sheep farmer from Waimate on the fringe of the Canterbury Plain. He was a thick-set, deliberate man; one of the oldest of *Viper*'s aircrew, and one of the most popular. He had been in the squadron for eighteen months now—a long time in days when the average life of an operational pilot was slightly under a year—yet he had never shot down a plane. He was too imperturbable to lose much sleep over this. Outwardly he treated his ill-luck as a joke; yet at heart he longed for the day when his guns would send a Heinkel or Junkers blazing into the sea. And this was not because of hatred or vanity or pride, but because he knew that he was already overdue for a shore appointment, and he wanted, before he left operational flying, to feel he had repaid in full the time and trouble and several thousand pounds spent on his training. 'I could never face my sheep again,' he once said to the C.O., 'if I don't get a single Jerry. "Brother," they'll say to me, "you might as well have stayed at home!" '

Adjusting his oxygen mask, he thought that this, surely, would be his lucky day. He glanced behind him and saw, tucked close behind his starboard wing, young Milton—the most junior of *Viper*'s fighter pilots. (The Wildcats always operated in pairs.) Blake motioned him further away; in the buffeting, uncertain wind there was no point in their aircraft keeping too close.

79

They levelled off at twelve hundred feet, just below cloud; then headed for the nearest group of planes. After a couple of minutes the Fighter Direction Officer called them up.

'Hello Jaybirds Two and Three. Bandits twelve o'clock. Sea level. Range five miles.'

They saw them almost at once. A single formation of Junkers 88, skimming the waves in loose echelon port.

They had rehearsed mock attacks so often that no signal was needed.

Milton peeled off. He eased the Wildcat into a thirty degree dive. Rapidly his speed built up: 260 knots, 280, 300, 320. A mile ahead of the Junkers he levelled off, close to the waves; then he headed straight for a plane in the centre of the formation. At a combined speed of six hundred miles an hour the aircraft hurtled together; head on. Gunfire from a dozen Junkers spat at the Wildcat, churning up and ricocheting off the sea; but Milton held his fire. A collision seemed inevitable. But at the last second the plane he was heading for began to wobble. Her pilot's nerve broke; he jerked back on his stick, and the Junkers rose sharply. Milton's gun-sight filled with the black under-belly of the plane. His finger tightened on to the firing button; tracer and cannon-shell ripped into the Junkers, tearing into her most vulnerable parts. At first she seemed quite unaffected. For three-quarters of a mile she rose in a steady, even climb. Then a small tongue of flame began to lick at her starboard wing-root. Suddenly, with a staccato cough, her fuel-tanks exploded, her wings broke off at the root, and through a haze of acrid smoke she spun screaming into the sea.

As Milton passed through the centre of the Junkers, Blake fell on to them from above and astern. Fire from their turrets came stabbing up at him, like lightning striking at an anvil; but he concentrated his attention on a single plane. At first the Junkers he headed for kept doggedly on course; then as the range closed, and his cannon-shell smacked into the bomber's wing, the German pilot swung aside. He almost collided with the plane beside him. Instantly the centre of the formation became broken up, with planes banking and wheeling away, as the Wildcat—guns yammering—flashed through the centre of them.

And before they could re-form Milton was diving on to them again, raking the sea ahead into a flurry of foam, forcing them to turn aside, away from the convoy, back towards the Norwegian coast. The formation broke up.

If they had kept together they would have had the safety of numbers. They would have suffered losses—two, maybe three would have been shot down; but by sheer weight they could have brushed the fighters aside and gone on to make a co-ordinated attack on the convoy. But they didn't keep together. They scattered. And individually they were vulnerable; vulnerable not only to the fighters, but to the ack-ack guns of the convoy. A few planes tried to re-form. But Blake dived on to them. Singling out their leader, he prised him out of the formation and drove him into cloud, smoke pouring from his starboard engine. Leaderless, the Junkers again scattered.

So it was that the warships guarding the convoy had to face not a massed co-ordinated attack, but a succession of individual planes, each of which ran in turn into a curtain of heavy fire.

Blake and Milton harassed them as far as the fringe of the convoy, then as the sky ahead darkened with bursting shrapnel, they wheeled aside.

And the German pilots found the fire of the warships as fierce and accurate as the fire of the fighters.

They hadn't expected as warm a reception as this. A few had already jettisoned their bombs, escaping the Wildcats; these slunk away. A few made half-hearted attacks, more intent on avoiding the gunfire than bombing accurately; their bombs fell wide. But most of the planes went in bravely; bravely but singly; and many of them were shot down.

Within twenty minutes of the Wildcats taking off the first group of aircraft had been beaten off; their losses, four planes shot down by gunfire and three by fighters. Their only success a number of near misses on a corvette, and a bomb which failed to explode lodged beside the funnel of a merchantman.

Blake and Milton didn't pursue the Junkers—for Milton's plane had been damaged. Instead they stayed close to the convoy. And it was as well they did. For the last of the bombers had barely disappeared into cloud, when a thudding of gunfire from the convoy's bow warned them that the second wave of attackers had arrived.

And this second attack was a very different affair from the first.

Blake saw the Junkers while they were still some miles from the convoy: a group of twelve planes in tight formation, coming in diagonally between the advanced screen and the forward vessels of the convoy itself. His first impulse was to drop on them at once; to join the pair of Wildcats already darting round them. But fighter pilots sometimes have a sixth sense; a fey awareness; a shadow of premonition. Blake had this feeling now. Strongly. More strongly than he had ever had it before. He felt the hair stiffening on the nape of his neck. He kept looking into his rear-vision mirror, expecting to see a Junkers on his tail. He stared again at the formation below. There were only ten of them now. The fighters had wheeled away; and every bofors and oerlikon in the convoy seemed to be hammering into them. He saw two more planes, like blazing torches, fall into the sea. But the remainder closed up and kept steadily on course. He realized suddenly that they weren't heading directly for the convoy; they were flying across its bow; drawing its fire. Again a shadow of premonition pricked up the hair on his neck.

The voice of the F.D.O., high-pitched and urgent almost split his earphones.

'Jaybirds Two and Three. To starboard. To starboard. Bandits approaching the stern of convoy. Sea level.'

The Wildcats flicked over into a half-roll. Their superchargers rose to a high-pitched scream as in a 400-knot dive they came flashing low over the rear ships of the convoy.

They were only just in time.

Blake was still turning his gun-button to 'fire', when a dozen Junkers burst out of a low belt of cloud and fell on to the hindmost ships. They had come in at sea level: too low for *Viper*'s radar to give more than a few seconds' warning. If the Wildcats hadn't been half-way to meet them the surprise would have been complete. As it was, Blake and Milton met them head-on, half-way between cloud and convoy; and the sudden clatter of gunfire from a new quarter gave the ack-ack crews a dozen precious seconds to re-align their sights.

Blake realized how much was at stake; realized what he had to do. He headed straight for the centre of the German planes.

He ran into heavy fire. Tracer from half a-dozen forward firing guns converged on to his plane. A spate of bullets tore through his starboard wing. Another burst smacked heavily into his engine. Dark-red banners of flame began to stream out of the cowling; a jet of oil sprayed thickly across his windscreen. But he held the plane on course. His finger clamped on to the firing-button.

Oil, dark and viscous, flooded across his windscreen. He was almost on top of the Junkers, when he felt the control-column judder. He moved it forward. Nothing happened. His ailerons had been shot clean away. Blinded and out of control, he slumped forward as the Wildcat scythed through the centre of the German planes. Two Junkers pilots straight in his path flung their aircraft aside. One touched wingtips with his neighbour. Instantly the two planes swung together. Clawing at each other like falling eagles, they spiralled seaward. Their bombs exploded; and they vanished in a haze of thin, acrid smoke.

Another Junkers, already damaged by Blake's cannon-shell, was flung half on to her back by the blast of the exploding bombs. Before the pilot could right her, the plane toppled into a spin. She was flying too low to have a chance of pulling out.

The Wildcat, blazing fiercely, bored through the last of

the Junkers. Flames from her engine trailed like torrents of blood in her wake. But Blake never felt the tongues of heat that cut like acetylene torches through the hood of his cockpit. For a burst of tracer had hit him, squarely and mercifully, across the heart.

The centre of the attacking force was broken. The arrow, its point blunted, momentarily lost way. Then the remaining Junkers began to close up. They had been slowed down, but they hadn't been halted. Once they had got their bearings, they again came sweeping on to the convoy.

Young Milton accounted for one more. Another disintegrated under the hail of gunfire that came flashing up from the warships of the screen. Half the attacking planes were down now; but the other half got through. Skimming the waves, weaving through the flak, they came screaming into the centre of the convoy.

Their target was the *Viper*.

One, banking to avoid a burst of tracer, feathered a wave with her wingtip. Instantly and without a sound, she flicked on to her back and plunged to the bottom of the sea.

Another, half-blinded by the streams of gunsmoke that drifted above the ships, mistook the *Atalanta* for the *Viper*. Her pilot went off at a tangent. The cruiser came swaying into his sights. At the last second he realized his mistake; but the *Atalanta* was a tempting target; his finger stabbed his release button. Four bombs fell seaward. Four pyramids of water welled up across the *Atalanta*'s wake, the nearest less than a dozen yards from her stern. She was flung violently forward. Her bows bit deep into an oncoming wave; and a thousand tons of ice-green sea swept foaming across her foredeck. Guns were torn off their mountings, lifelines snapped like rotted twine, and twenty men, the life beaten out of them, were sponged off the cruiser's deck. Her screws were flung high out of water. She shuddered violently in a terrible, vibrating spasm. Then, shaking the water off her decks, she rose slowly out of the sea and settled reluctantly

on to an even keel. But her propeller shaft had been twisted and strained; almost at once her speed began to drop.

From *Viper*'s bridge Jardine saw the last four planes come sweeping towards the carrier. They came in very low, almost brushing the sea, and very fast. One, hit by oerlikon fire, was forced away, trailing smoke. But the others got through. Their bomb-doors opened. A dozen 500-lb. bombs patterned the carrier.

Viper disappeared.

Around her the sea heaved skyward. On every side great pyramids of foam leapt high above her flight deck. Sheets of driven spray swept her decks; bomb splinters knifed into her hull. But by a miracle she wasn't directly hit. She jerked and quivered, vibrated and shuddered, as the force of the explosions lifted her half out of the water. She reeled sickeningly into the vast craters bitten out of the sea—Jardine thought for one terrible moment she would roll completely over—but at last, as the bomb-splashes subsided, she emerged into clear water. Then, like the *Atalanta*, she settled slowly on to an even keel.

All over the ship men picked themselves dazedly up. And the first thing they noticed was the silence.

Gone suddenly was the scream of planes; gone the clatter of machine-guns, and the bark of bofors and oerlikons. The sky was clear. As suddenly as they had come, the Junkers had disappeared.

In the sudden quiet Jardine heard all the small, familiar sounds of his ship: the wind whining through the radar screen, the hum of the air-conditioning plant, the creak of ice caught up by the slackened arrestor wires, the hiss of the bow wave foaming along the keel. They were very dear to him. Then, rising above these, he became conscious of another not-so-welcome sound; the dull roar of the still-increasing gale.

He sent a signal to every ship in the convoy: 'What damage? What claims?'

It was some time before all the replies came through. But the first few signals he received had a heartening similarity, and they set the pattern for those that followed. When all the replies had come in Jardine found that the balance was better by far than he had dared to hope. German losses had been heavy; twelve Junkers destroyed and eleven damaged: a third of the attacking force put out of action. His own losses had been amazingly light. One Wildcat had been lost, and one damaged. Of his merchantmen only one had been hit—and that by a bomb which had failed to explode. Of his warships, *Viper*, *Atalanta* and a corvette had suffered near misses, and a destroyer had been hit flush on her for'ard turret. But warships are built for punishment; the damage in each case was repairable and within a couple of hours the ships were back to near-maximum efficiency.

For most people the battle ended with the disappearance of the last of the Junkers (this was an hour before sunset). But *Viper*'s Wildcats were still in the air; and for the fighter pilots and for the batsman the real battle was still to come.

.　　.　　.　　.　　.

When young Jardine had been carried below by the doctor, he was so deeply asleep that even when the carrier rolled sharply and the doctor lost his footing and half fell against a bulkhead, he never opened his eyes. The doctor took him to his own cabin. He laid him on the bunk, pulled off his boots, loosened his clothes and covered him with blankets. He would have liked to give him an injection—to put him under for twenty-four hours—but he knew that young Jardine would soon be needed again for the job that only he could do. He sat down beside him and took his pulse. It was a hundred and twenty.

The doctor stayed in the cabin for a couple of hours; but young Jardine didn't wake; not even when *Viper* reeled and juddered under the hail of bombs. Several times he moved uneasily in his sleep; once his face puckered up, his tongue ran from side to side across his mouth, and his lips began to move. The doctor bent over him. At first the mumbled words were meaningless; then suddenly he got the gist of them. He straightened up: surprised.

It was a few minutes after this that a steward knocked on the cabin door. He brought a message from the Captain: would the S.M.O. report to his sea-cabin right away.

.　　　.　　　.　　　.　　　.

Jardine's sea-cabin was small and austerely furnished: two chairs, a bunk, a fitted cupboard, a steel safe. Jardine was sitting in one chair; he motioned the doctor to the other.

'You've been with my son?'

'Yes, sir. I have.'

'How is he?'

'All right at the moment. He's asleep.'

Jardine nodded as if reassured.

'I want you,' he said, 'to keep an eye on him.'

The doctor studied his finger-tips. It was some time before he replied. Then he said slowly:

'I'll do what I can, sir. But what he really needs is sleep.'

Jardine got up and began to pace the cabin.

'He'll have,' he said, 'to do without sleep. As long as the convoy needs planes, he'll have to keep going.'

'If you drive him too hard, he'll crack up.'

There was an awkward silence. At last Jardine said:

'I don't enjoy doing this. He is my son, you know.'

'And if I'm to keep an eye on him he's my patient. I'm telling you, sir, as a doctor. Take some of the strain off him, or he'll crack.'

For a long time Jardine was silent, then he said:

'I'll do anything you say—short of stopping flying.'

'Thank you, sir.' The doctor leaned forward. 'Then what I'd suggest is this . . .'

.　　　.　　　.　　　.　　　.

When young Jardine felt the water splashing on to his face, he dreamed, in the second before he woke, that his

88

mother was playing with him in the bath. He was three, and far too young of course to lie on his back by himself; but she had had one hand under his head, and the other hand was squeezing a sponge, and the water was cascading over his tummy, up round his neck and over and across his forehead; and she was laughing. Then the water splashed into his mouth. He woke, and saw the doctor, holding a dripping flannel, standing beside his bunk.

He lay quietly on his back, the happiness of his dream ebbing away like a rip-tide laying bare the mud flats of an estuary. There's no holding the tide, he thought. The past is another world; another and better world. He sat up.

'What is it?' he said. 'More planes?'

'There will be soon. But you've some time yet: a good half-hour.'

'This isn't my cabin.'

'No. It's mine.'

'What happened?'

'You fell asleep. It was partly exhaustion; partly lack of food. You've not had a proper meal for days. My steward's bringing one in a minute.'

The meal, when it arrived, consisted of a bowl of steaming soup and a plate of ham, egg and chips. Jardine took a spoonful of the soup. He laid the spoon down and looked at the doctor.

'It tastes funny,' he said.

'Funny? How?'

Jardine tasted it again.

'Sort of dusty. You try.'

The doctor sipped at a spoonful.

'Seems all right,' he said, 'to me.'

Jardine had been watching him carefully. He got off the bed, picked up the bowl and emptied it into the wash-basin.

'You've been talking to my father,' he said.

'That was rather a waste, wasn't it?'

'You've been talking to my father. He asked you to see I didn't crack up. So you thought you'd drug the soup.'

'There was a mild sedative in the soup. Nothing more.

If I'd wanted to drug you, I'd have given you an injection while you were asleep.'

Jardine looked at the plate of food.

'I suppose,' he said, 'you've doped the ham and eggs as well?'

The doctor sighed.

'Listen, Bats,' he said. 'You don't have to try to be tough. You've got a vital, terribly exacting job. Naturally, people want to help. If they try to give you a hand, don't slap them in the face.'

Young Jardine's anger died.

'I'm sorry,' he said. 'I know I'm being difficult.'

He sat down and started to eat his ham and eggs.

'It's just,' he said, 'that I can't stand being watched.'

'Being watched?'

'Being watched by Father. For twenty years I've felt him "keeping an eye on me". I know what he's afraid of. I know he thinks I'm a coward.'

Fear and love, the doctor thought; like the ivy and the honeysuckle, they choke each other to death.

'You're wrong,' he said. 'When you talk like that I almost wish I had given you a sedative.'

Young Jardine stood up.

'Later.' He tensed his legs against the swaying of the ship. 'The storm's getting worse,' he said. 'Soon there'll be no flying. No landing-on. Then you can give me all the sedatives you like.'

.   .   .   .   .

His three hours' sleep had done him good. He felt almost refreshed as he clambered up to the crewroom to collect his bats. He heard the trumpet of the tannoy, 'Stand by to land-on two Wildcats'; he felt *Viper* heel over as she swung into wind; he quickened his step.

Except for Marsden the crewroom was empty.

'Ah, Bats!' Marsden seemed glad to see him. 'I've got three messages for you.'

'Before I land the Wildcats?'

'Yes. Your father thought you ought to see the latest wind report.'

He handed Jardine a printed slip: *Wind west-north-westerly* (it read), *50–55 knots. Gust of 65–75 knots. Backing and increasing slowly. Frequent squalls of snow.*

Young Jardine handed it back.

'Very encouraging,' he said.

'The other messages are more cheerful. Your father says you can take your time with the landing-on. He's turned the whole convoy into wind. He doesn't mind how long the landings take.'

'Now that,' said young Jardine, 'really is a help.'

'The last message is a bit personal. I know these things aren't usually talked about, but I think you're being recommended for a gong.'

'A gong? Whatever for?'

'For your batting, of course.'

'Good God! What a crazy idea! Whatever will Father say?'

'As a matter of fact,' said Marsden, 'it was his idea.'

Walking down the flight deck young Jardine looked about him. No prospect could have been more desolate: grey sea, grey sky and a frenetic wind. But happiness, he thought, isn't a matter of where you are. He had never been happier than now. The fact that he'd been recommended for decoration—probably the M.B.E., Marsden had said— meant very little; it was the fact that his father had done the recommending that pleased him beyond words. He can't, he thought, think so badly of me after all.

He wasn't foolishly optimistic about what lay ahead—a glance at *Viper*'s round-down rising and falling among the waves dispelled any idea that his job would be easy—but he felt within himself the glow of a new-found confidence. His father had faith in him. He had something to live up to now. In the morning he had landed fifty planes; surely in the afternoon he could manage six.

He clambered on to the batting platform, nodded at the

Flight Deck Officer, and the first of the Wildcats was signalled in.

But the storm had worsened since the morning; and Wildcats were never as easy to land as Swordfish. The first plane Jardine had to wave off seven times. Seven times it came curving in. Seven times, as it hung poised to land, the carrier corkscrewed away. And seven times, as Jardine waved it off, it quivered away from the batting platform, its undercarriage almost feathering the deck. The eighth approach was a ragged, untidy affair—Jardine realized the pilot must be desperately tired—but at the last moment the plane steadied-up; and, as it neared the round-down, the flight deck rose obligingly. Jardine gave the signal to cut and the plane thudded down, heavily but safely, on the last arrestor wire. Her hook caught at once, and she was jerked to a stop.

Two dozen of the flight-deck handling party came swarming out of the catwalk. They seized hold of the plane, man-handled it for'ard, and lashed it down in front of the barrier, so that the deck was clear for another plane to begin its approach.

The next five landings, which would normally have taken perhaps ten minutes, went on for over an hour. Time and again one of the Wildcats would make a perfect approach, only for the carrier to corkscrew away at the last moment, leaving the plane half-stalling fifty feet above the deck. Those were the worst moments of all: the moments of terrible uncertainty when Jardine had to send a plane round again, and the engine would burst into screaming protest, and the plane would rise with uncertain and agonizing slowness away from the steeply pitching deck.

Once, as Jardine gave the signal to cut, *Viper*'s stern rose with extra violence; the landing-wheels of the approaching fighter thudded on to the edge of the round-down; the plane bounced thirty feet into the air. For a second it hung poised over the barrier—nothing it seemed could prevent it crashing into the parked aircraft—then the pilot rammed open his throttle. Slowly, uncertainly, the Wildcat picked up speed; but not enough speed. It lost height, it sank quivering over the carrier's bows and disappeared into the trough of an enormous wave. It seemed as though it could never rise again; but as *Viper* breasted the next swell, the men who had rushed to the rails saw it was still airborne, its flaps almost brushing the sea. And at last, very slowly, it began to climb to safety. It circled the carrier and started its next approach.

At the end of half an hour two Wildcats were safely down. At the end of an hour, four; and a few minutes before sunset the miracle was repeated for the sixth and final time as the last of the fighters thudded safely on to the flight deck.

Behind the stormclouds, the sun sank into an angry sea. Soon it was night.

.   .   .   .   .

By three o'clock it was utterly dark. At least, Captain Jardine thought, one danger has passed: there'll be no more attacks from the air; the weather is too bad. He returned *Viper* to normal routine.

In theory the danger from U-boats still remained; but as he looked at the tempestuous sea, Jardine doubted if any submarine could launch an attack in conditions such as these. (The wind was now a steady sixty knots, increasing fast; and as the storm centre approached, the wave-crests drew farther apart, and heightened.) He decided the weather was too bad to keep his anti-submarine patrols in the air; when the Swordfish now circling the convoy had finished her patrol, he'd cancel flying.

But half an hour before the plane was due to return she called the carrier up. She reported a U-boat contact fine on their starboard bow. Should she, she asked, investigate?

No message could have been more unwelcome. Quickly Jardine called for detailed weather reports and for the exact range and bearing of the U-boat. Then he paced the bridge, alone, wondering if the chance of sinking the U-boat was worth the risk of losing the plane. (And the risk was a very real one; for the submarine had surfaced dead down-wind, and the wind was increasing fast; if the Swordfish went after her and got too far to leeward, she might never return.) He decided to take the risk—hadn't Churchill said that the sinking of a U-boat had an equal effect on the course of the war to a thousand-bomber raid on Berlin; and the thousand-bomber raid wasn't made without risk.

What happened in the next hour was to haunt Jardine for the rest of his life.

With the gale behind her it took the Swordfish only a few minutes to home on to the U-boat. Jim Heywood, the pilot, had hoped his attack would succeed by surprise; for in the worsening storm the U-boat captain would hardly expect a plane to be airborne. But his hopes weren't fulfilled. At the last moment the U-boat dived; and by the time Heywood's starshell illuminated the sea she had disappeared. For a couple of minutes he tried to circle the spot where she had vanished, hoping she would surface; but his plane was like driftwood, caught in the flood of a swollen river. He felt himself being driven off course, battered eastward by hammer-blows of wind. He decided to give up. He turned the plane westward, and headed back for the convoy. But after a quarter of an hour they seemed no nearer; indeed his observer's A.S.V.X. screen indicated that if anything they were losing ground: the speed of the wind was greater than the speed of the plane, and they were being forced backward, away from the carrier, out into the empty sea.

There is a saying that God helps those who help themselves. It isn't true. If ever a man fought for his life—fought with courage and skill—it was Heywood. He jettisoned his depth-charges; he threw out his ballast—he pushed home his over-ride and increased speed to 100 knots. He went down to sea-level, hoping the wind there would be less. And for a little while it seemed that his struggle would not be in vain. For very slowly the plane began to close with the convoy.

In the Operations Room Stone watched Heywood's progress on his radar screen; watched the shadow of the plane as almost imperceptibly it inched closer to the convoy. At last it was very near; less than five miles from *Viper*'s beam. For half an hour it clung there motionless, clawing its way head-on into the insensate gale. Then, as the wind increased, it began very slowly to fall back. On his screen Stone watched the shadow grow gradually smaller, gradually more indistinct; until at last it faded utterly away. What a terrible way, he thought, to die.

That evening Jardine divided his time between the bridge and the radar screen. He looked at the shadow of the Swordfish several times; but he only mentioned it once —quite early on—to ask if the Swordfish had enough petrol to get her to Norway.

'A pity,' he said, when Stone told him she hadn't.

The Air Operations Officer, and several others, thought him callous; thought him cold and unfeeling. Just what they expected him to do, they couldn't have said themselves. Perhaps they would have been mollified by a display of public grief. Perhaps they thought he ought to have behaved like the hero of a melodramatic film; to have gone about with tight lips and haunted eyes. But Jardine failed to oblige them. He made no apologies. No excuses. He had, to all outward appearances, no regrets. He simply carried on with his job.

As soon as the Swordfish had vanished from the screen he went back to the bridge. He stayed there a long time, watching the warning signals of the approaching storm: the shriller screaming of a wind that backed gradually from north to west; the more violent swinging of the pendulum that measured *Viper*'s pitch and roll; and the increased distortion of radar screens, now darkened out by the great sheets of water torn in continual cataracts from the crest of every wave. And as the storm-drenched hours passed slowly by, he found that his mind started to wander away from the present—over which he had no control—and his thoughts, following an all-too-familiar pattern, turned to the past, and he began to think of all the pilots and observers for whose death he had been responsible.

There were, he reminded himself, a great number of them; far too great a number for him ever to sleep happily again. There had been a time when he could remember all their names; but lately his memory had begun to fail him; and this, quite illogically, distressed him. But their faces he still recalled with clarity. They welled up now, one after another, out of the midnight sea: Dewhurst with his pint tankard of beer; Hunt with his eternal pipe; Maitland with the photographs of his wife and children. They were the substance of his secret thoughts, the men who walked the sequence of his dreams, the ghosts he could never lay.

Viper, nearing the storm centre, moved uneasily under his feet. He made an effort to throw off his depression. Why, he asked himself, think of the past? They had been brave men. Now they were dead. If he wept till the oceans overflowed he couldn't bring them back to life. His job was with the future; the future of his convoy.

His heart warmed at the thought of his convoy. Already they had been through much together. They had been battered by U-boats and planes; they were about to be battered by the approaching storm. But they were coming through. And not a single merchantman had been lost. Nor, he thought, will they be lost. Though I lose everything else, I'll not lose them.

He felt a gentle, persistent pulling at his arm, and looking round saw Ian MacLeod. He took the midnight met. report, and saw that the storm centre was now only fifty miles ahead, and that at its vortex the wind was estimated at 130 miles an hour.

7

AFTER he had landed the last of the Wildcats, young Jardine went below. He took his sedatives willingly, almost gratefully, like a man who welcomes oblivion. For now he could sleep, sleep deeply, knowing that for many hours no hand would come plucking at his shoulder, no voice would be telling him to get up and land the planes. He climbed into his bunk; his eyes were shut before his head had touched the pillow.

When he woke he felt relaxed and at ease. Lying in a contented haze, on the borderline of wakefulness, he looked lazily at his watch. The hands pointed to close on ten o'clock—he supposed in the morning. So he had slept for seventeen hours; no wonder he felt a stir of hunger. He rolled out of his bunk; the deck fell away from him and he was thrown violently to the floor. Picking himself up, he realized that *Viper* was reeling and corkscrewing with a frightening malevolence. So they were near the vortex of the storm.

It took him half an hour to dress, and by the time he staggered across to the wardroom breakfast was being cleared away. The meal was cold (for there was no heat in the galley) and rather like an obstacle race; a pursuit of bread and butter and marmalade across a wildly tilting table. Sometimes *Viper* rolled so violently that the plates jumped over the fiddles—the partition-boards designed to keep the food in place.

From the way the ship was behaving young Jardine had

some idea of what it would be like on deck; but he was unprepared for the tumult that flung itself on to him, as an hour later he clambered into the catwalk. He stood appalled, clinging in disbelief to the stanchions of a companionway—to have ventured on to the flight deck itself would have been suicide. What frightened him most was the way the world had shrunk, had shrunk during the night to a tumultuous square mile of wind and sea and sky.

The sea had been tempestuous before. Now it had taken on an elemental fury, an insane malevolence. Huge waves, a mile and a quarter from crest to crest, came thundering in endless succession out of the west. Each as it neared the carrier towered high above her; each, it seemed to Jardine, must engulf her utterly. Yet always *Viper* rose; always she climbed the steepening incline, until the wave-crest trembled beneath her and was passed. Then came the plunge, the sickening, breath-catching plunge, down, everlastingly down, to the pit of the next cavernous trough. Sometimes, as Jardine watched, he saw the whole crest of a wave ripped away by the wind, and flung horizontally across the sea. Those were the worst moments of all; the moments of terror, when ships in the path of the avalanches of water reeled and staggered as thousands of tons of wind-driven sea sluiced through their upper-decks, crushing gun-mountings, tearing off carley-floats, buckling deck-houses and funnels, and sweeping men, before they had time to cry out, into the frenetic sea.

And the sea was not alone in its fury; it had a companion in violence, a partner in destruction: the wind. It came clawing out of the west. It filled Jardine's ears with a continual high-pitched roar. And it, like the sea, could pick up a man; could hurl him across the deck, could smash him lifeless against gun-turret or deckhouse, or sweep him like a splinter of flotsam over the side.

Above them, the sky hung low, a livid dead-white, as though wiped clean of colouring or cloud. It was an evil, unpitying sky, as charged with malice as either wind or sea.

In storms such as this, thought Jardine, ships can founder, can disappear without a trace.

For half an hour he clung to the companionway, sodden, frightened and cold. I'll stay here, he thought, until I stop trembling. I'll not go below, afraid. He forced himself to watch the waves as they flooded in like mountains blotting out the sky, and the gulfs as they opened up beneath like caverns torn out of the sea; until at last he realized that for some reason beyond his comprehension *Viper* was neither going to turn turtle nor stand on her head; then his fear, very gradually, began to ebb away.

After a while he thought of looking for the rest of the convoy.

He could see them only occasionally: a solitary merchantman poised at some fantastic angle on the slope of a mountainous wave, or a warship riding the horizon on a surge of spume and spray. Their tortured antics were hardly reassuring; but at least it was something to know that other ships in the convoy had survived the night.

The same thought brought a touch of comfort to his father, who had spent the last thirty-six hours wedged into the least windswept corner of the bridge. For most people in the carrier the end of flying had meant the end of responsibility; but for Captain Jardine the problems of the night had rivalled those of the day.

At midnight he had ordered the convoy to reduce speed to five and a half knots, just enough to give his vessels leeway and keep them steady on course. Three hours later, when wind and sea were still increasing, he had reduced speed still further, and ordered the convoy into more open formation. He had also told the vessels to show navigation lights—since there was no fear of attack. But not until dawn, when they were nearing the inner core of the depression, did he give the order that every ship had been longing for; then at last he turned into wind, turned the convoy head on to the threatening sea. After that, there was nothing more he could do.

Until that morning his ships had been able to keep some sort of formation. Gone of course were the neat parallel columns that five days before had drawn away from the Shetland assembly box; but up to now the convoy had always been a manageable whole. But as the depression centre rolled toward them, and wind and sea built up to a climatic fury, the convoy began to break up.

Jardine fought desperately to keep his ships together— for he could look ahead, could visualize the return of better weather and the coming again of planes and U-boats (they would have an easy job if they found the convoy scattered). Besides, he and his vessels had come in the last few days to know and respect each other; they had been proved in the same furnace, hammered into cohesion on the same anvil; each vessel that now dropped out was like a friend departing for a far country—a friend who might never be heard of again.

First to go was one of the smaller merchantmen. She found that even the reduced speed of four knots was more than she could manage. She began to drop astern. Jardine did all he could to keep her with him. He sent her encouraging signals, caustic signals, blasphemous signals. He reduced the whole convoy to two and a half knots—but at this speed *Viper* was sluggish in answering her helm; twice she was thrown broadside on to the mountainous seas, twice she rolled almost to destruction. It wasn't, Jardine knew, worth risking the carrier to save the merchantman. There was only one thing he could do. He ordered the convoy back to four knots. The merchantman fell gradually astern.

Next to drop out was a corvette. She had been damaged in the previous day's attack—the plates in her bow having been strained in a near miss from one of the Junkers. Now, under the pounding of the sea, her rivets began to shake loose; beads of water formed inside her bulkheads; a watertight compartment was flooded, but still the moisture came seeping in. After a hurried exchange of signals, the corvette turned her undamaged bow to the waves and went limping southward. A week later she staggered half-sinking into Rykjavic.

The convoy was being whittled away.

At noon they suffered another and far more serious loss. The *San Antonio* signalled *Viper* that her engines were running hot, she suspected a blocked oilpipe. Jardine swore softly. What a time, he thought, for a ship to get her innards choked up! His anxiety was heightened when he remembered that the *San Antonio* was one of the ships carrying the crates of special equipment. But there was no help he could give, no advice he could offer; he simply acknowledged the signal and waited. After half an hour the merchantman signalled again:

'Request permission to stop engines and heave-to for repairs.'

So there, thought Jardine, is the end of the *San Antonio*. In a sea like this she'll founder. But he could only trust her Master's judgment; he didn't query his request; and he kept his fears to himself.

'Permission granted,' he signalled. 'But cool your ardour as soon as possible. Tonight you'll have to sleep alone.'

He watched through his glasses as the merchantman lost way; watched as she fell astern, her engines silent. Almost at once she yawed broadside on, and began to roll scuppers under.

Three ships lost, he thought, in as many hours. Soon there'll be no convoy left.

The storm showed no sign of slackening.

After a couple of hours yet another merchantman signalled that she was falling gradually astern. It was then that Jardine decided to split the convoy up; half would heave-to, the other half would stay under way.

It was the smaller ships he left behind: four merchantmen, four corvettes and two of his older destroyers. In charge of them he left the *Atalanta*; and the anxiety of parting was lessened by the knowledge that he couldn't be leaving his ships in better hands.

Limping slowly among the white-crested waves the

vessels sorted themselves into two groups, one surrounding *Atalanta*, one surrounding *Viper*; the former hove-to, the latter ploughed on.

It was the large vessels that stayed with Jardine; the vessels that needed speed to answer their helm: two cruisers, four destroyers and four of the larger merchantmen. For a couple of hours they laboured on, moving slowly, under a sky that became steadily darker as the storm-centre drew near. And still the wind increased; still the sea rose. This can't, thought Jardine, go on; nothing can stand up to punishment like this; something will have to give.

He was right.

The *Denver Willis* was a nine thousand tonner; the only American-built vessel in the convoy, the only ship whose plates were not riveted but welded. So far she had stood up to the seas well, with little sign of strain; but a hull that is welded is far more vulnerable than one that is riveted, and now, without warning, a complete section of the *Denver Willis*'s bow buckled in.

Half an hour before sunset the Yeoman handed Jardine a signal.

'*Denver Willis* to C. in C. Plates buckling on starboard bow. Am turning stern into sea.'

In spite of the risk, Jardine reduced speed. He watched the *Denver Willis*, a clean-lined ship a little astern of *Viper*, back slowly into the vast rollers. For several minutes she seemed to be riding normally. Then the First Lieutenant muttered that she looked a bit low in the head. Jardine nodded. He too had seen that she was down by the bows and listing slightly to starboard.

The Yeoman brought him another signal.

'*Denver Willis* to C. in C. Plates continue to buckle. Have sprung series of uncontrollable leaks.'

Jardine knew then that the merchantman was doomed. Courage could not save her, nor seamanship, nor skill. What the sea wants, it takes. But though he knew this, he fought for the *Denver Willis* with a reckless disregard of the cost. He risked the convoy to try and save her.

He ordered his ten vessels to heave-to. Signals flashed from ship to ship, and soon a cruiser and a destroyer began to manœuvre upwind of the listing merchantman. Moving cautiously through the heavy seas, they inched towards her. Soon they were close—dangerously close, for already the *Denver Willis* was out of control, yawing and plunging about in sudden, unpredictable swoops. But close as they were, the warships couldn't get near enough to shoot life-lines from ship to ship. Only one hope remained. They began to jettison oil. Thick viscous streams pulsated out of their pipelines and almost at once the wave-crests began to flatten. They jettisoned enough oil to have ironed any normal sea to the smoothness of a millpond; but oil was their lifeblood; they could spare only so much; and what they could spare was not enough. The crests of the waves were smoothed out; but the great rollers themselves were unaffected; their angry impact continued; and soon the *Denver Willis* began to settle by the bows.

There are some things that can never be forgotten. As he watched from *Viper*'s bridge, Jardine reminded himself that every day of every year far greater tragedies take place than the loss of a single merchant vessel in a storm. Yet never before had he felt such pity and despair, never such anger and impotence as when that evening in the gathering darkness he saw the *Denver Willis* being bludgeoned to death by the uncaring arctic waves.

She lay in the centre of a storm-lashed circle of ships. All of them watched her; none of them could help her. Her bows dipped lower. Her list increased. It ought, thought Jardine, to be night; this is something that shouldn't be seen. He shut his eyes as she fell on to her side; a great wave rolled toward her; and when he opened his eyes she was gone.

It was quite dark by the time the convoy got under way.

There was one survivor from the *Denver Willis*: an engine-room artificer from Cardiff; and a long time afterwards he told the crew of the destroyer that picked him up something of the miracle of his escape.

He said that when the master of the *Denver Willis* realized the oil was having no effect, and that the sea was too rough for boats to be lowered or lifelines shot aboard, he told his crew their only chance of survival was to lash themselves to a piece of wreckage and jump overboard; there was, he said, a million to one chance that they would be flung against one of the ships that lay down-wind. This to the artificer seemed good advice. So he lashed himself to a lifebelt; and the lifebelt he lashed to the side of a packing-case. Then with three or four others he was among the first to jump. He jumped at a carefully chosen moment, as the *Denver Willis* was rising on to the crest of a swell. He hit the sea feet first, and at once felt himself glissading downward and forward along the reverse side of the swell. His packing-case acted as a sort of surf-board, and he entered the water surprisingly smoothly. The sea, he said, didn't strike him as being especially rough; but it was cold; so cold that almost at once he lost all feeling in legs and arms. He had the sensation of being carried forward at a great pace by a half-frozen underwater current. He had no control whatsoever over his speed, direction or position in the water; and it was quite by chance that he found himself smashed suddenly against the hull of a ship. And draped against the hull were the rungs and guide-lines of a scrambling net. For several seconds he lay spreadeagled against the hull, pinned down by the pressure of the sea. His hands froze on to the rungs of the net. Then the great waves bludgeoned him unconscious. But still he clung there, frozen solid, a part of the net itself. Twice the ship rolled him beneath the waves; then he was seen, and the net was hauled aboard.

They had to cut through the rungs of the net, because his hands couldn't be unclenched from them. They had to saw through the planks of the packing-case, because he was frozen solidly on to it. Then they took him below, and cut off his clothes, and put him into a bunk and made him sick, to cough the oil out of his lungs. They gave him all the blankets and all the warmth and all the care they could;

and though for two days he hung very near to death, in the end he lived—the only survivor from the S/S *Denver Willis*.

As though the sinking of the merchantman had been its last insensate gesture of malevolence, the storm that evening began to lessen. It lessened slowly; so slowly that its slackening could be measured only by instruments and not by sense. But the instruments did not lie, and that night the wave-crests fractionally lowered and the wind grudgingly dropped. By midnight the waves had fallen to fifty feet, and the wind to a mere ninety knots.

But the night brought problems of its own. For now, as the centre of the storm passed, the wind began to shift. It shifted capriciously, swinging at random between west and north. And the waves, whipped up by the wind, shifted too; so that to the steady march of rollers out of the west was now added a northerly cross-chop. The night became full of treacherous surprises; full of unlikely waves that came crashing out of the darkness; full of sheets of spray that pitted into the ships from unexpected quarters. In the uncertain sea the helmsmen needed all their watchfulness, all their skill, to prevent their vessels being flung broadside on.

Viper became especially unmanageable—for an aircraft-carrier with her overhanging flight deck is at the best of times an unstable vessel. Twice she was flung beam on to the heavy seas; twice she rolled to the very limit of her safety margin. Then, in the small hours of the morning, she came very close to foundering.

For some time she had managed to meet the waves head on, and Jardine was beginning to think she had weathered the worst of the storm, when a little before dawn a sudden shift in the wind caught her on the bow. She yawed off course. She fell away into an approaching trough. At the bottom of the trough she toppled into an unexpected hollow, a little whirlpool of scooped-out sea. Before she could answer the helm she swung broadside on. The approaching wave was not an especially large one; normally

106

Viper would have ridden it safely and swung back into wind; but suddenly the crest of the wave was ripped away; ten thousand tons of water were peeled off, were flung like an avalanche against the side of the carrier.

Viper was smashed on to her beam.

For ten to fifteen seconds she hung there, waterlogged and helpless, on the verge of turning turtle. The seas swept green across her flight deck; they crushed her down; they beat her low into the water. All over the ship lashings parted; lifelines snapped; and stores, drip-trays, ammunition boxes and men were flung to the deck. Then the wave passed. Abruptly the avalanche of water was cut off. Slowly and unwillingly *Viper* heaved herself back to an even keel. She met the next wave on her bow, the next head on. For the moment she was safe.

Men picked themselves dazedly up. In bridge, engine-room, mess-deck and store, damage was quickly assessed. Everywhere it was found to be superficial; everywhere except in the hangar.

From here came a cry for help; a cry that was desperate and urgent; a cry that brought fear, turning like a knife at Jardine's bowels.

.   .   .   .   .

The hangar of an aircraft-carrier looks to the uninitiated like a random parking-ground of planes, each of which is ensnared in a casually woven spider's web. But the experts know better. To them each plane is scientifically and accurately placed; and the 'spiders' webs' are ropes, guide-lines and hawsers, all of which are arranged with mathematical precision to withstand the greatest possible strain. In bad weather these lashings are increased in size and number, until the planes look like embryo cocoons, and the hangar is criss-crossed with a closely woven maze of ropes. It would seem impossible, under the weight of so many ropes, for anything to move an inch.

Now, after twenty-four hours of storm, the Senior Air

Engineer Officer, Commander Aplin, was still keeping the hangar personnel at work, checking and tightening the lashings. For he knew that if a plane did somehow work itself free it could easily be flung the length and breadth of the flight deck, smashing and crippling whatever lay in its path, turning the squadron in a couple of minutes into a knacker's yard of scrap.

So hour after hour riggers and fitters had been crawling among, over and under the planes, lashing down control surfaces, tightening ringbolts, doubling and then trebling every rope, hawser and guide-line. And they did their work well.

When *Viper* was flung on to her beam, the strain on the ropes securing the planes was unbelievable. But in the whole hangar only one parted. By ill-luck this was an especially vital one; a lashing which held down the tail-plane of a damaged Swordfish. As *Viper* heeled over, the lashing, with a snap like the crack of an elephant whip, parted; its end seared into the hangar bulkhead; a little spiral of smoke floated upward; and the tail-plane swung free. The ropes holding the fuselage tautened under the added strain. For a second they held; then with reports flung like rifle-shots around the hangar, they too were ripped apart. With a grinding wrench the plane shook herself free; with gathering momentum she slithered across the canted deck; with a shuddering jar she smashed into the aircraft parked beside her.

A dozen ratings who had flung themselves at the Swordfish in a vain attempt to hold her were tossed aside, like spray from a feathered oar. One shattered his knee-cap and rolled screaming into the scuppers; one lay inert, his head lolling sideways at an unnatural angle.

Aplin stood appalled. He saw some men rushing towards the plane, others rushing away from it. He heard a confused medley of sound; orders and counter-orders, cries of pain and fear.

He snatched up a megaphone.

'All hands! All hands!' His voice flooded out like the

108

roar of a foghorn. 'Muster in Bay Eleven. Hold that Swordfish fast. Pin her against the bulkhead.'

The shouting died; the mêlée sorted itself out, as from every corner of the hangar men began to claw their way for'ard to grapple with the breakaway plane.

Aplin snatched up the telephone that connected him with the bridge. He spoke urgently to Jardine, and a second later the Captain's voice came sharply over the ship's tannoy.

'Emergency! Emergency! Port watch muster in the hangar. At the double! Repeat at the double!'

Once again the Swordfish slithered across the deck, flinging off a handful of men. Once again it splintered into the neighbouring plane. Then, as it swung back against the bulkhead, three dozen ratings flung themselves on to it. With shoulders arched and muscles cracking they fought to hold it, to pin it against the hangar wall. On the shifting deck they slipped and slithered; they were flung against stanchions and bulkheads; they were trampled underfoot. But they held their ground. They could never have done it alone; but with every second more men—the port watch brought racing to the hangar by Jardine's emergency call—hurled themselves into the fray. Some got a hand to the plane, others packed up against the first men's backs, forming a chaotic rugger scrum, a scrum that by sheer weight of numbers held the Swordfish fast.

As quickly as it had come the crisis passed. What remained to be done—the re-securing of the Swordfish and the neighbouring plane—would be difficult; difficult and dangerous. But Aplin knew it could be done.

An hour later he was able to report to Jardine that the planes were safe; that the hangar was back to full efficiency.

But he was taking no chances. He divided his personnel into two watches. One he kept constantly on duty—officers, petty officers and ratings alike—working their way round the planes; tightening, checking and double-checking every nut, ring-bolt and hawser.

All that night they kept it up, crawling about on hands

and knees, squirming under wing-roots, peering with torches into dark recesses, working their way endlessly round, up, over and across each of the lashed-down planes. At first the novelty of the work outweighed the discomfort; but after a couple of hours the novelty began to wear away. Several men, caught unawares by a sudden pitch or roll, were flung sharply against plane or bulkhead; several more were violently sick, their stomachs outraged by the sweet, sickly odour of oil that clung, close and cloying, to the planes. It was dirty, exhausting, cramping work. At 8 a.m. the watches changed over; and for a few hours ropes were tightened and bolts screwed home with a renewed energy and precision. But soon the new hands became as tired and cramped and trembling as the old; and as dawn found *Viper* still riding out a storm of little-diminished fury it began to seem to those in the hangar that they could not remember a world that consisted of anything else but bolts and ropes and straining planes, seen dimly through a sweat-wet haze of cramp and tiredness and pain.

. . . . .

But at least in the hangar it was warm; which was more than could be said for the bridge, where for the last forty-eight hours Captain Jardine had remained, self-locked into the least windswept corner.

The cold and damp had long ago seeped through his sea-boots into the muscles of his legs; the wind and spray had long ago numbed his fingers to unfeeling stalactites of ice. But still he stayed there, hour after hour, immobile as though he were frozen solid, a part of the ship herself.

Every now and then he saw, swinging across the back-cloth of night, a tiny red or green navigation light. For perhaps a second it would burn clearly; then some unseen mountain of water would rise between them, and the light would disappear. But it was comforting to know that some ships at least were still with him.

At ten o'clock MacLeod brought up the morning met. report. Jardine found it difficult to read. His eyes, sore and inflamed, refused to focus. He handed the report to the Officer of the Watch.

'Read it, please,' he said.

The Officer of the Watch shone his torch on to the printed sheet.

'*December 9th,*' he read. '*Dawn report.*'

Dawn! thought Jardine. And sea and sky so dark that ships in the next column can't be seen. . . .

'*The centre of the depression has now passed over the convoy, and is moving rapidly toward the Norwegian coast. Strong northerly gales will continue throughout the morning, decreasing slowly p.m. As the wind drops, there will be a temporary improvement in conditions ; then as the cold front passes over the convoy, cloud will again thicken and lower ; heavy snow blizzards will develop in the evening.*

Grade 'C' forecast till 2200/9.

WIND	Northerly: 70–80 knots; decreasing slowly.
WEATHER	Fine in late morning and early afternoon: snow blizzards in late afternoon and evening.
CLOUD	7/10 at 1,000 feet, rising and decreasing temporarily; then increasing to 10/10 and lowering to 300 feet in the late afternoon.
SEA	Heavy northerly swell, decreasing.
OUTLOOK FOR TOMORROW	Gale gradually dying out as the depression moves eastward. Wind and sea decreasing; snow will end abruptly during the night.'

'Thank you,' Jardine said.

He put the report into his pocket, and anchored himself again into his corner of the bridge.

After a little while he saw that the colour of the eastern sky was changing. It was no longer black, but a pale anaemic grey. It was dawn. The start of another day in the convoy to Murmansk.

.   .   .   .   .

That morning the weather began to improve. The greatest improvement was in the wind; it no longer screamed; it merely roared; and it had lost the power to rip away whole patches of the sea. Soon the cloud base rose, the sky lightened, and visibility improved; by noon all ten of the larger vessels were in sight. Jardine called MacLeod to the bridge.

'Where,' he said, 'is the snow?'

'It will aye be coming, sir.'

Jardine looked at the rising sky.

'God forgive you,' he said, 'if you're wrong. I won't.'

'Aa'll noo be wrong.'

Soon the sky was lighter than it had been for days. The First Lieutenant and the senior officers of Jardine's staff waited impatiently for him to signal the convoy to re-assemble; but Jardine made no signal; he watched the sky.

It was two o'clock before the strata of whitish cloud began to darken. It darkened first into long, wind-torn ribbons of grey that streaked horizontally across the sky; then the ribbons thickened and merged, darkened and lowered; they turned into little patches of turbulent cloud; and from these there came the snow.

It came at first in sudden, isolated squalls, with tiny brittle flakes that were more like hail than snow. Then, as the cloud patches became lower, darker and thicker, the flakes became heavier and moister, and the squalls more frequent. By three o'clock *Viper* was pitching into a full arctic blizzard; the cold front swinging out of the north behind the depression centre. Visibility dropped to zero.

Keeping together had been difficult in the storm; in the blizzard it wasn't to be thought of. Jardine did the only possible thing. He broadcast a coded message, and the last of his ships—vessels that had clung together through day after day of ordeal by bomb, torpedo, wind and sea—broke apart. With their navigation lights invisible and their radar sets unworkable, the risk of collision was too great for them to stay together. The ten ships fanned out; five, ten or fifteen degrees away from the mean line of advance.

Soon they were pitching into utter darkness: blindly, gropingly, alone.

As the winds of autumn strip petals from a dying flower, so that evening the blizzard shredded away the last remnants of Jardine's ships. The convoy, as a convoy, simply ceased to exist.

.   .   .   .   .

But the vessels kept in touch by radio.

Jardine had thought carefully about the pros and cons of using their radio. Should he stay in contact with his ships, knowing that every signal he made would be picked up by German listening posts; or should he ban all transmission, leaving both his own vessels and the Germans in the dark? He decided that no matter what the cost he must keep in touch with his ships; and having made this decision, he put no limit to the number of signals sent. Indeed he encouraged his ships, especially the stragglers, to report every two or three hours, giving their estimated position, course and speed, and a brief report on their seaworthiness and weather.

These signals brought, during the night, a glow of comfort to the storm-driven vessels. Though battered to near-exhaustion, though shrouded in perpetual darkness, the signals told them they were neither forgotten nor alone. Even in their isolation they felt watched over, cared for. The radio made the night less dark, the storm less frenzied, the thought of the morrow more endurable.

Soon after the blizzard started Jardine went below. For the moment there was nothing he could do, and he hadn't slept for the last three days. But he left orders to be woken the moment the snow eased off.

For eight hours the snow fell steadily. Then abruptly it stopped. At one moment *Viper* was pitching into a veil of darkness, the next she had broken out into a sky that was moonlit and clear. Occasional patches of cloud were racing low over the sea, stars of gemlike brilliance were reeling across the sky, and fairy lanterns, violet and silver and blue, were dancing above the northern horizon: the *aurora borealis*. Here, in the wake of the storm, the night was touched with a wild, tempestuous beauty; only the wide-spaced rollers, surging endlessly south-eastward, retained their original menace.

Jardine, now back on the bridge, took stock of the situation.

His first need was to fix *Viper*'s exact position. The dead reckoning plot showed her a little below the seventieth Parallel and some four hundred miles from Norway. But in the last few days accurate navigation had been impossible. He doubted if the plot was accurate to within a hundred miles.

With a good deal of difficulty the Navigating Officer took an astral fix. This showed the carrier well above the seventieth Parallel and four hundred and sixty miles from Norway.

The First Lieutenant pinpointed a spot midway between the two positions.

'I suggest we say we're here, sir. Until we get an accurate fix.'

'Yes.'

Carefully Jardine wrote out their estimated position on the back of a signal pad. He did a quick calculation; then called the Yeoman of Signals.

'Pass this,' he said, 'to all vessels. My position at midnight,' he glanced at his pad, 'will be 002.47° West; 70.30° North. My speed 3 knots. My course 350°. Report your estimated position and close with me at dawn.'

After the signal had been sent, Jardine and the First Lieutenant paced the bridge. How many ships, Jardine wondered, would reply? Of those that did reply, how many would be able to close by dawn? He knew that the better weather would mean renewed attacks by U-boats and planes, perhaps by surface forces as well. Unless he gathered them in, his ships would be picked off one by one; the most distant stragglers would be the first and easiest victims.

It was the best part of an hour before all the replies came

in. Then the news was better than Jardine had dared to hope. All the escorts, and all the merchantmen but two, had acknowledged the call; and two-thirds of them said they could close by dawn.

Jardine called a staff conference. Together with *Viper*'s senior officers he studied a chart of the north-eastern Atlantic. If their calculations were right, their ships would reassemble close to where the sea-bed rose to form Jan Mayen Island and the North-East Jan Mayen Ridge. They were, Jardine noted, a good deal to westward of the track they had been routed by; and they were forty-eight hours behind schedule. But that didn't trouble him.

'The important fact is,' he said, 'we're over half-way to Murmansk, and so far we've lost only a single merchantman.'

'Pretty good,' the First Lieutenant said, 'considering.'

In his heart Jardine agreed; but he knew the danger of over-confidence. He rapped sharply on the table.

'To business, gentlemen,' he said. 'Let's not congratulate ourselves too soon. Let's remember we haven't got a convoy at the moment. The question is, how are we going to re-assemble it?'

8

JARDINE didn't like staff conferences. He kept them as short as possible, collecting information rather than opinions, making decisions rather than discussing them; and no one was surprised when the gathering of senior officers broke up after less than twenty minutes. They had discussed the weather conditions; they had pinpointed the assembly area; they had fixed the position of all their ships but two. The one thing they hadn't discussed was the basic problem that all the others led up to: how to reassemble the convoy. That was something Jardine wanted to decide alone.

He went below to his cabin to think things out. One problem worried him especially: should he use his aircraft to search for and bring in the stragglers? Was it worth risking his planes to save his ships? It was a difficult decision to make. Thinking of the losses his squadron had suffered already, he shivered. He felt suddenly very tired; tired and uncertain and old. The problem seemed insuperable. After a while he called through to the bridge and spoke to Halsey.

'I want to see you, the C.O. and Bats,' he said. 'My cabin, right away.'

When they came, he regretted having called them. He wasn't used to asking for help.

He had arranged four chairs round a table. On the table was a chart, a sheet of tracing paper and the latest met. report.

'Sit down,' he grunted, when the last of the three had arrived; nervousness, they noticed, made his manner unusually abrupt. 'I want your advice. First I'll give you the facts.' He smoothed out the chart. 'The convoy is scattered now, but I've ordered a rendezvous for dawn. Soon some twenty ships ought to be converging on this assembly area' —he pointed on the chart to a spot a little north of Jan Mayen Island. 'Is that clear?'

The others nodded.

'Now what I expect to happen is this. At dawn some fourteen or fifteen ships will be near the assembly box. Visibility will be good; with a little help from the corvettes these ships should come together; then there's safety in numbers; they can look after themselves. But some five or six ships will be missing. They are the ones I'm worried about. The ships that are lost or are lagging astern. The stragglers.

'Now the problem is this. If we were a large convoy, I'd send corvettes to search for the stragglers and bring them in. But we're not a large convoy. If we'd a full squadron, I'd make *them* search for the stragglers; but we haven't a full squadron. If the weather was good, I'd risk flying the few planes we have; but the weather isn't good.' He paused. 'Now you're the experts on flying. That's why I want your advice. You know the circumstances. Now would you or wouldn't you use the planes?'

There was a long silence; then Halsey asked how many stragglers there were likely to be.

'And,' added Marsden, 'how far astern are they?'

Jardine smoothed out the piece of tracing paper and superimposed it on the chart. On it the position, course and speed of every vessel was clearly marked; a cross for warships, a circle for merchantmen. Most of the crosses were reasonably near the assembly box; but several of the circles were far astern—one by as much as ninety miles—and another was nearly as far to starboard.

'And two ships,' said Jardine, 'haven't answered yet. God knows where they are.'

Young Jardine looked at his father. He felt suddenly disillusioned. Was this the man who had taught him to make his decisions alone, the man who walked by himself, the man he had looked up to as an acolyte to his God? It struck him—like a physical blow—that his father was an old man. His disenchantment turned to pity; but it was a pity without understanding. It is true that he realized something of the strain his father was facing; he understood a little of the loneliness of authority, the burden of command; but he thought his asking for help was a sign of weakness, a confession of failure.

Halsey and Marsden understood the position more acutely. To them Captain Jardine was a man who had run temporarily out of courage. They knew that each man has so much courage he can draw on; so much and no more. They knew that when courage dies, all dies; and that a man left without courage is like an empty shell. What can such a man do? Sometimes he breaks under the strain; sometimes he runs away; sometimes he borrows courage from others. Some men ask God for courage; Jardine was asking his friends. Halsey and Marsden were at once pleased and disturbed: pleased that Jardine should have come to them, disturbed at the prospect of added responsibility. Because they liked as well as respected the Captain they gave him no glib answers.

For a long time nobody spoke. Then Halsey said, quite simply:

'The squadron will suffer losses, but I think the planes ought to be flown.'

'I wouldn't feel happy,' young Jardine volunteered, 'about landing the Wildcats. Not in a sea like this.'

The Captain looked at Marsden.

'It's your squadron,' he said, 'what do you say?'

'I think we should rule the Wildcats out. I agree with Bats there; the weather's too bad to land them. We've got eight Swordfish left. Half of these I'd keep in the hangar; we'll need them later, when we get to Kola Bay. The other half I'd use to round up the stragglers.'

There was a short silence, then Jardine said:

'Thank you—all of you—for helping me.'

He began to fold up the chart. Halsey half-rose, thinking the conference was over, but Jardine motioned him to sit down.

'One last point,' he said. 'It's over forty-eight hours since there was any flying. Until a plane takes off, we won't know how bad conditions are; so the first plane off will run a rather special risk. I don't think a crew ought to be detailed off for a job like that. Perhaps, Marsden, you'd ask for volunteers: volunteers for a test flight?'

'Yes, sir. I'll do that.'

'I'd like to see the pilot and observer before they take off.'

'Very well, sir.'

'There are some pilots I wouldn't want to go.'

'I see.'

'Yourself, for instance.'

Beneath the table Marsden's hands tightened. 'Surely, sir, a C.O. has some privileges.'

Jardine's voice was sympathetic. 'I know,' he said, 'just how you feel. For years now I've been asking men to do things I can't do myself. That's one of the bugbears of a senior rank. The simple fact is this. You're more use to me alive than dead. I'll not let you go on a job some other pilot could do equally well.'

He stood up.

'I want a crew ready to take off an hour before dawn. Halsey, see they report to me on the bridge.'

The conference broke up.

.   .   .   .   .

Through the night signals pulsated out, as every hour the ships of the convoy reported their dead-reckoning position to the carrier. As the weather improved, navigation—especially astral navigation—became easier, and the vessels were able to fix their positions more accurately. Those that had fallen astern increased speed; those that had been driven sideways, closed in. Soon Jardine and the First Lieutenant were able to visualize the pattern of the convoy as it would be at dawn.

The ships were drawing together well; remarkably well. Of their twenty-two vessels, all except one had now reported their position; and fifteen of them seemed likely to be in or near the assembly area by sunrise. That left six vessels to be rounded up. Of these, only two gave Jardine real anxiety: the *Empire Malcolmson* and the *San Antonio*. The former was heading off at a tangent, straight for Norway: either her steering was damaged or her navigation was badly at fault. The latter was the ship that had dropped out of convoy with a blocked oilpipe; this had taken twenty-four hours to mend, and now the *San Antonio* lay far astern, a lone ship wallowing in the wake of the convoy; the answer to a U-boat's prayer. And she had aboard the crates of special equipment.

These two, Jardine decided, were too far away to be brought in by surface forces; they would have to be found and escorted back by air.

.　　　.　　　.　　　.　　　.

At seven o'clock the squadron were called to the crew-room, and Marsden asked for volunteers: volunteers for a weather test, to be followed if conditions were good enough by a search for the *San Antonio* and the *Empire Malcolmson*.

'I don't want you to volunteer as crews,' he said, 'but as individuals. We'll put pilots' names in this cap, observers' in that. The first name drawn out of each will form a crew.'

While he was talking, young Jardine handed round slips of paper.

'If you want to volunteer,' Marsden ended, 'write your name on the paper; if you don't, leave it blank. In either case fold the paper up and drop it into a cap.'

He left the room. When he came back he was glad to find that the first two slips he pulled out had names on them.

The caps were emptied out of a port-hole; the slips of paper fell fluttering into *Viper*'s wake; and there to all outward appearances was an end to the business of volunteering. But for one man things didn't end there; for one of the pieces of paper had been blank.

The first name out of the observers' cap was Kit James; the first out of the pilots', Vic Saunders. They reported to Jardine on the bridge, then went below for breakfast and briefing while their plane was brought on deck.

An hour later they took off in the pale half-light of dawn.

Viper was pitching heavily, and the take-off had to be timed to a split second—a fraction too soon and the Swordfish would follow the down-tilted deck into the sea; a fraction too late and she would crawl along the up-tilted deck and stall over the bows; the result in either case would be fatal. Saunders's timing was good; and the plane had reached her take-off speed by the time the upward thrust of *Viper*'s bows flung her into the air.

Then came the time of uncertainty, as Saunders and James began their weather test. Jardine watched anxiously from the bridge. Would the wind, he wondered, be too strong for them?

For twenty minutes Saunders circled the carrier. The wind was strong and blustering; but not so strong he couldn't keep the Swordfish under control. He flew north, south, east and west. He flew at three hundred, five hundred and a thousand feet, and found a wind at each height. He flew through cloud and under cloud. He reported on turbulence and icing. And when Jardine had studied the figures that were radioed back, he smiled and said the weather was good enough for flying.

Then the rounding up of the stragglers began. A second Swordfish, that had been waiting on deck, took off to search for the *Empire Malcolmson*, and Saunders and James disappeared downwind on their search for the *San Antonio*.

They knew that she wouldn't be easy to find. Her estimated position (and it could only be a very approximate one) was eighty-five miles due south of the carrier. This put her dead downwind; and with a fifty-knot gale behind her the Swordfish soon reached the spot where the *San Antonio* should have been.

She wasn't there.

Visibility was good—fifteen to twenty miles. They ought, thought James, to be able to find her. But he knew that in less than an hour they must be heading back for the carrier; for into wind, the return trip would take far longer than the outward. They dropped markers and smoke floats and found an exact wind; then they began a square-search. At the end of half an hour there was no sign of the *San Antonio*, nor after forty minutes, nor after fifty. The minutes passed; their petrol drained away; and still the A.S.V.X. screen shimmered white and empty; no smoke-smudge darkened the empty canvas of the sea.

James switched their radio to intercom.

'We ought to be heading for home, Vic.'

'Whenever you say.'

'Are you O.K. for another ten minutes?'

'If you are.'

'Right. Another ten minutes it is.'

They had time to finish one more leg of their square search. Half-way through it James saw on his screen a faint shadow at a range of twenty miles. They turned towards it. Soon Saunders saw a starshell fall golden into the sea. And a moment later they sighted the *San Antonio*.

For two days the merchantman had been alone, her only contact with the world a crackling, impersonal radio. Alone she had spent twenty-four nightmare hours rolling beam on as she repaired her oilpipe. Alone she had ridden out the blizzard. Alone she had struggled through the night to close with the rest of the convoy. It had begun to seem to her crew that they would be alone for ever. Then out of the alien sky came the Swordfish.

As Saunders swept low over the merchantman, her crew came tumbling on deck. They capered, shouted and cheered; they waved oilskins, lifejackets and flags; an Aldis flashed incoherently from the bridge.

But for Saunders and James joy at finding the San Antonio was tempered by anxiety over their petrol—they should have been heading back for the carrier this last quarter of an hour. Quickly James flashed the merchantman by Aldis:

'Sorry we can't stay. No petrol. Your correct course to close with convoy is 024°. Repeat 024°. Another plane will be with you soon.'

The Swordfish banked away; before the San Antonio had started her reply she was heading for home.

The first thing James did was to give Saunders a course —028°. He didn't tell him their lives depended on how accurately it was steered, for that was something both of them knew. Then he called up Viper and reported the San Antonio's position—now the merchantman had been found she could be given cover until she caught up with the convoy. After that there was nothing more he could do; nothing but check and recheck his plot, and listen to the rhythmic beat of their engine and the dull roar of the head-wind. They had been airborne now a little over two hours. The endurance of a Swordfish was slightly over four hours; which meant they had roughly two hours left to cover the eighty-odd miles back to the carrier. It would have been easy without the headwind. After checking his plot for the fifth time James estimated that if all went well they would reach Viper about ten minutes before they ran out of fuel.

After three-quarters of an hour he tuned up his A.S.V.X. On the flickering screen the convoy stood out indistinctly at a range of forty-five miles. Their course looked accurate.

'I think,' he said to Saunders, 'we're going to make it.'

But a few minutes later a message came through from Viper. The radio operator's voice was clear and cheerful.

'Hullo Seagull Five. Treetop calling. Radio silence will come into operation forthwith. At 12.15 convoy is leaving the assembly box. Course 023°. Speed 5 knots. If you have any message pass it now.'

James was silent. He felt a slow paralysis creeping over

him, as if his blood was congealing to ice. It was several minutes before he switched his radio to transmit.

'Hullo Treetop,' he said. 'We've no message for you.'

He looked at his watch. In a few minutes the convoy would be under way. They wouldn't be getting under way without cause—probably, he thought, they'd been spotted. But why in God's name, he asked himself, did they have to move off on a course of 023°, dead away from him, so that every turn of their screws took them so much further from his plane? He realized they would never catch up with the carrier now. Somewhere astern of the convoy the last drop of their petrol would be drained away.

·　　·　　·　　·　　·

Back in the carrier it was one of those mornings when everything goes right.

A few minutes after the first Swordfish had disappeared to search for the *San Antonio*, challenge and recognition signals were exchanged with a warship fine on *Viper*'s bow. It was the *Atalanta*—for a terrible moment Jardine had thought from her silhouette it was the *Brandenberg*—and she had with her a merchantman and two corvettes. The latter, much to their captains' disgust, Jardine sent off to round up the nearest stragglers; then beneath a gradually paling sky he settled down to wait for his ships to reassemble.

They came slowly, hesitantly, one by one; limping in like storm-drenched animals creeping back to shelter. Most of them showed signs of their ordeal by storm; some had especially terrible scars. One of the corvettes was badly down by the stern, and her after-deck lay buckled, almost stove-in. One of the merchantmen was listing heavily; her bridge, crumpled by the full impact of a wave, lay half-flattened aslant her deck. Another had her funnel knocked sideways, and was belching sporadic clouds of smoke. They were a scarecrow armada; battered, salt-caked, ice-encrusted; but Jardine was happy to see them, happy as if they had been the most powerful and majestic warships.

One ship he was especially glad to see: the *Valeriana*: the vessel that hadn't replied to his signals. Now as she came labouring in from the south, she flashed the carrier by Aldis that she was undamaged except for her radio, which was smashed beyond repair.

By ten o'clock eleven vessels had reached the assembly box. Jardine began to feel, once again, that he was in command of a manageable body of ships. He thought the sea was probably too high for U-boats to attack. But he was taking no chances. He kept the vessels zig-zagging round the four sides of a square; and he kept an A/S patrol orbiting the assembly box. Young Jardine had plenty of batting now. But his two days' rest had refreshed him. In spite of the mountainous seas, he landed the planes safely.

By eleven o'clock sixteen vessels had come in; and by noon the miracle had been achieved: within twelve hours of the blizzard's ending, all Jardine's vessels but two were back in convoy; and these two—the *Empire Malcolmson* and the *San Antonio*—had both been found, and were being escorted back.

The *Empire Malcolmson* was on the convoy's bow. Jardine wasn't worried over her; she could cut across to join him; by nightfall she should be back in station. It was the *San Antonio* that he was anxious for. She was sixty miles astern. He couldn't wait for her indefinitely; and when the convoy did get under way, their course for Murmansk would take them directly away from her. Another difficulty was that to give her continual and separate A/S cover would tax his few remaining Swordfish—not to mention his batsman— to breaking point. If he had to keep two patrols in the air, his already depleted aircrew would be forced to fly three hours, rest three hours and then fly again; and that sort of routine was more than flesh and blood could stand.

He cursed and grumbled at the *San Antonio*. He sent her a spate of signals urging her to increase speed, ordering her to close more quickly. But he never thought of leaving her. She was the ninety-and-ninth of his sheep. Somehow, no matter what the cost, he would bring her back.

He had just made up his mind to wait for her till night-fall, when the Yeoman handed him a signal: a U-boat contact from the patrolling Swordfish. A few minutes later the vibrating thud of depth-charges rolled among his ships. His assembly area had been found. His convoy had been rediscovered.

He couldn't risk waiting now; he couldn't stay in the assembly box while planes and U-boats massed for an attack. He reimposed radio silence; then reluctantly, a little after noon, set course for Kola Bay. But he didn't desert the *San Antonio*; he didn't leave her alone. He sent back a des-troyer to keep her company, to make the coming night less lonely; and he decided he'd keep an aircraft over her as well.

The convoy got under way. They stood north-eastward. The waves were steep and grey-green; the wind was east and razor-sharp; the sky was white and cold as marble. Jardine was glad to be on the move. Now, once again, each turn of their screws was taking them nearer to Mur-mansk; another three days, he thought, and we'll be there.

Then he remembered Saunders and James.

His gladness ebbed suddenly away. Sea and wind and sky took on a bleaker aspect. How many more of my squadron will die, he thought, before this convoy is over? He looked at the uncaring waves and shivered. He looked at his hand, clasping the bridge-rail, and saw it was trembling. Inside his brain there began a strange flutter-ing: the wing-beats of an imprisoned bird. Suddenly he spun round. He snapped open a voice-pipe.

'Captain here, Stone. How long has that Swordfish been airborne?'

'Saunders, sir? Three hours twenty-five minutes.'

'If we hold course, will he get back?'

'No, sir. I've just been working it out. He'll ditch about fifteen miles astern.'

Slowly Jardine put the voice-pipe down. Astern of the convoy were a pilot and observer whose lives he held in the balance. If he kept on course, they would die; if he turned back, they would live. He knew what he ought to do: to turn the convoy round would be to endanger the lives of some eight thousand men, to risk the loss of twenty-three ships and a hundred-thousand tons of supplies—not to mention the secret equipment. Judged by any yardstick it was a risk that couldn't be justified. He saw very clearly what he ought to do.

But he turned the convoy round. He headed back for the assembly box.

Twice in the next half hour the roll of depth-charges echoed among the zig-zagging ships. Once a destroyer, mistaking a cloud-shadow for a Junkers, loosed off her ack-ack. Nerves were laid bare. No good, it was felt, would come of turning back. Jardine was asking for trouble.

He knew it was true. He knew it wasn't a well-calculated risk he was taking. It was a surrender to sentiment. Impulsive. Uncharacteristic. Without justification. It was a gamble that didn't deserve to pay off.

By the time they got back to the assembly box the Swordfish had been airborne four hours. It would be too ironic, thought Jardine, if she didn't find us now. He looked at his watch. The minutes passed; four hours five minutes; four hours ten minutes.

Then, low on the southern horizon, the Swordfish was sighted, only a few feet above the waves.

Viper swung into wind. A sudden quietness spread over the flight deck as plane and carrier converged. Every second was precious now. As he watched from his batting platform young Jardine could hear, in his imagination, the engine stuttering as it sucked in the last cupfuls of fuel.

Saunders didn't bother about an approach, he lowered his arrestor hook and came sliding on to the flight deck in an awkward, skidding turn. His petrol, young Jardine realized, must be registering zero. It was no time for conventional doubts. He held his bats level. He made no signals until the plane came crabwise over the round-down; then in one movement he straightened her up and gave her the signal to cut. She plummeted down, heavily but safely, on the last of the arrestor wires. And as she taxied for'ard of the barrier, her engine gave three choking coughs and cut, stone dead. When they looked in her fuel-tanks they found there wasn't enough petrol to cover an upended sixpence.

Nothing succeeds like success. Because it had ended happily, many people told themselves that Jardine's return had been justified. But he knew better. Never again, he told himself. Miracles don't happen twice.

    .   .   .   .   .

All afternoon the convoy moved northward into a lessening head sea. Jardine expected to be attacked. He kept his ships closed up at action stations. But of planes or U-boats there was never a sign.

At two o'clock the *Empire Malcolmson* rejoined them. All his ships except the *San Antonio* were back in convoy now. The Germans, he and Halsey agreed, by not attacking while the convoy was scattered, had missed their opportunity. For this, MacLeod told them, they must thank the storm-centre which was now lashing the Norwegian coast, preventing the aircraft from taking off and the U-boats from leaving harbour.

They used their unexpected breathing space to good advantage. That afternoon, in merchantmen and warships, the damage caused by the storm was repaired. Equipment was tested and tuned-up; guns were lubricated and re-aligned; decks were hosed clean of ice. And in *Viper*'s hangar Aplin achieved a minor miracle; the two shattered Swordfish were dismantled and their undamaged parts combined into a single serviceable plane; a phoenix that rose slowly from a welter of useless scrap.

And all the while one Swordfish circled the convoy and another the *San Antonio*. Plane after plane took off, flew its two-hour patrol, landed-on, was refuelled and re-armed, and then took off again. And soon it was twilight.

The day died angrily in red and ebony, with a great

haloed sun, framed by cumulus, turning the sea into a field of blood. Jardine looked at the sea, the innocent, treacherous sea. He suspected it was not as empty as it looked. He suspected (though he could get no proof of this) that from far astern a U-boat had been shadowing them, was shadowing them still. A little before dark he altered course to the east; he hoped the U-boat had seen; later, when it was quite dark, he would increase speed and swing back to the north.

At four o'clock he handed over to the First Lieutenant and went below. On the way to his cabin he looked into the Ops Room. His son was there, cat-napping again between patrols, though with an aircraft to land every hour he got only a few minutes' sleep at a time. The dark circles under his eyes, the captain noticed, were coming back.

He checked the exact position of the *San Antonio*. She was less than forty miles astern. She ought, he reflected, to be all right with a plane and a warship to guard her. By dawn she should trouble him no more, she should have caught the convoy up. She was, he and Stone agreed, a lucky ship. Not many vessels ploughing a solitary course in the wake of a convoy would have survived.

They didn't know that even as they were talking the *San Antonio* was fighting for her life.

.   .   .   .   .

In spite of the storm, six reconnaissance aircraft had managed to take off from Mosjoen; and it was one of these —a Blom and Voss seaplane—that sighted the *San Antonio*. She sighted her at twilight, as the merchantman's silhouette stood out sharply in the path of the setting sun; and an easy victim she looked. The German pilot set his bomb-release switches to live, and eased into a confident dive.

Then he spotted the Swordfish. Mistaking her for a patrolling fighter, he pulled hurriedly back into cloud. Emerging cautiously from time to time he studied her silhouette; he couldn't understand why she was moving so slowly. Then he identified her. A Swordfish! Here was no terrible fighter armed with machine-gun and cannon; only an unarmed, obsolescent biplane with a speed even slower than his. His confidence restored, he left the cloud and came diving down on the merhantman. He was a little disconcerted to see that the Swordfish had taken up a position between him and his target. But how, he asked himself, could an unarmed biplane hope to stop him?

The same thought was puzzling Marsden and his observer, who for the last ten minutes had been watching the Blom and Voss with alternate amusement and dismay.

'Alas!' Marsden observed, as at last the German pulled away from the cloudbank, 'he's recognized us. See how bravely he's coming on!'

He headed straight for the seaplane. They met midway between merchantman and cloud. Tracer came spitting at Marsden, but he bucketed beneath it, and the two planes hurtled together, head-on. The German pilot was young and inexperienced. He thought he was going to be rammed. Frightened, he flung the seaplane aside. His first run-in had been thwarted.

The Blom and Voss banked ponderously round. As she started to come in again, a ragged burst of ack-ack cracked out from the *San Antonio*'s single bofors. The shells burst extremely wide. Marsden, who had no high opinion of Merchant Navy gunfire, looked round in alarm. The sea, he noticed, was darkening; but not quickly: not quickly enough. He realized that his was a forlorn hope, a lost cause. Once or perhaps twice he might frighten the seaplane off, but not indefinitely. The best he could hope for was to delay the inevitable; perhaps if he delayed it long enough darkness would make the attack more difficult, or perhaps the destroyer (which he knew Jardine had sent) would come to his aid.

The second time the Blom and Voss came in she tried to by-pass the Swordfish by diving round her, down to sea level. Marsden headed her off, and at the last moment cut suddenly in front of her and dropped two of his depth-charges. Twin pyramids of water leapt skyward, straight in the German pilot's path. Spray and falling water blotted out the merchantman. Again, angrily, the German flung the seaplane aside. His lips tightened. He'd stand no more interference. He'd settle with the Swordfish first. But when he looked round for her, she was nowhere to be seen.

'Herr Leutenant!' the alarmed voice of his navigator crackled in his earphones. 'She's close behind us. On our tail.'

Outraged, he flung the seaplane round the darkening sky, twisting, banking, diving, side-slipping. But still the Swordfish clung there. It was unthinkable that he couldn't shake her off; a challenge to his superiority; an affront to his dignity. He opened full throttle, and toppled the seaplane into a long, screaming dive. His air-speed built up; a hundred-and-twenty knots, a hundred-and-forty, a hundred-and-sixty. The Swordfish began to lag behind; far behind. The German pilot was elated. He hardly noticed where his dive was taking him.

Aboard the *San Antonio* the bofors crew held their fire as, less than a mile to starboard, the seaplane came sweeping down on a course near-parallel to theirs. Then as she came beam on they opened up.

The first salvo burst straight in front of her nose.

The German pilot had forgotten the merchantman. Startled, he swung aside, swung straight into the second salvo, which, clean as a bill-hook topping nettles, scythed off the seaplane's tail. Engines screaming, the great plane toppled seaward. She entered the water neatly, with hardly more spray than is made by a plummeting skua; and no trace of her was seen again.

Soon afterwards it was dark.

As the sun set, the sea changed colour. It changed from green to grey, from grey to amethyst, and then from amethyst to black. Over the darkening waters Marsden flew low, his Aldis winking congratulations at the *San Antonio*. But he couldn't believe that the affair had really come to an end. The Blom and Voss was destroyed. There was no doubting that. But had she, Marsden wondered, radioed her base; had she, before she was shot down, passed back the *San Antonio*'s course and speed? If she had, the Germans would have a pointer to the position of the convoy; and they would know that in the convoy's wake was a tempting target: a solitary, unguarded merchantman.

Marsden's fears were well-founded. For the seaplane had in fact broadcast not only to Mosjoen but also on the secret U-boat frequency; and a little to eastward of the *San Antonio* a submarine that had surfaced to charge her batteries picked the message up. She was ideally positioned for a night attack. As the sun set, she went down to periscope depth and began to head for the *San Antonio*. Her navigation was good. Slowly their tracks converged.

.   .   .   .   .

It was nine o'clock that evening when Haysom and Tregoning took off in bright moonlight. Theirs, it was hoped, would be the last patrol to cover the *San Antonio*.

As they headed for the merchantman, now less than twenty miles astern, Haysom was silent. He was thinking; and his thoughts were far from happy; for the blank piece of paper dropped that morning into the volunteering cap had been his. Ever since, he had tried to think of other things; of his parents, of his home, of the Purbeck Hills he loved; but all these were shadows now, unsubstantial things, the memory of them blotted out by the image of a piece of paper on which he had failed to write his name.

Moonlight slanted into the cockpit, lighting up the dials of his instrument-panel, gleaming on the knuckles of a flying-glove clenched too tightly on to the control column. Whatever happened, Haysom thought, Tregoning must never know what he had done; though he could no longer respect himself, at least he still could warm himself a little in the glow of the man who admired him.

He heard Tregoning give him an alteration of course. Automatically he banked the plane on to its new heading and a few minutes later they found the *San Antonio* and began to circle her at a range of ten miles.

And at much the same time the U-boat that had been converging on the merchantman since sunset picked her up on its hydrophones. Cautiously she surfaced. She spotted the *San Antonio* at once, a dark smudge on the moonlit horizon; she saw the destroyer, too; then her radar picked up the patrolling plane. Swiftly she submerged down to periscope depth.

The U-boat Commander realized his task wouldn't be easy. But he was skilful and experienced. He stalked the *San Antonio* with patience and cunning. Hour after hour he edged cautiously in, a few yards at a time, while the moon reeled silently among the clouds, her silver light falling impartially first on hunter, then on hunted, then on a wingtip of the circling plane.

It was four hours before the Commander made his attack. He chose his moment well, when destroyer and plane were both on the far side of the *San Antonio*, and the merchantman was silhouetted clearly in a pathway of moonlit sea. Then he moved in: in little submerged rushes; three hundred yards under water, then up to periscope depth. The *San Antonio* grew larger in his sights. She swung beam on. At last she filled the whole of his viewfinder.

It was five months since the Commander had claimed a sinking. This time he intended to make sure. To be doubly certain of the merchantman's exact course, range and speed he surfaced—for less than the third of a minute. Then he launched his torpedoes: a salvo of six.

They were well aimed.

He snapped the periscope down. The U-boat crash-dived. Her crew listened eagerly for the muffled explosions. But they listened in vain. The minutes passed. They began to move uneasily. Then the splitting roar of a depth-charge turned their expectancy to terror. A second explosion flung them to the deck. The lights went out; there was a noise of ripping metal, and the hiss of sea-water flooding into their hull. The U-boat was flung to the surface. For perhaps a minute she floated there, inert as a stunned salmon. Then, as she began to settle on an even keel, her conning-tower was flung open and her crew came tumbling on deck.

It was a hundred-to-one chance that saved the *San Antonio* and crippled the U-boat. In the few seconds that the latter had lain on the surface, Tregoning happened to be measuring his distance and bearing from the merchantman. As the U-boat surfaced and the echo came welling up on his screen he was able to calculate her bearing in a flash. He shouted the bearing to Haysom. The plane banked sharply round and headed for the U-boat. Her course took her directly over the *San Antonio*. The second she was on course, the echo began to fade. Tregoning realized what was happening; realized the U-boat was diving, her torpedoes fired. The Swordfish was passing over the *San Antonio* now. With sudden inspiration he unhooked his Very pistol, leant out, and fired it over the merchantman's bow. A cascade of starshell burst in front of her. Sensing danger, but not knowing its whereabouts, the *San Antonio*'s master spun over his helm. The vessel heeled over; and as she swung head on to the U-boat, a look-out gave a great cry of fear.

'Torpedoes!'

If she hadn't been turning already the *San Antonio* would have made her last voyage. As it was, more by luck than judgment, she combed the torpedoes exactly. One passed a dozen feet to port; another brushed foaming past her beam—so close that the look-out saw little flecks of spray, flung from its warhead, spatter against their hull. Then the torpedoes were past.

The *San Antonio* gave a startled belch of smoke. Then, at full speed, zig-zagging crazily, she fled. And five hundred yards in her wake the Swordfish flung herself on to the disappearing U-boat.

Haysom dived in fast. The U-boat herself had disappeared; but her slick—the little circle of churned-up sea where she had dived—remained; and into this fell two of Haysom's depth-charges. Twin pyramids of water heaved into the sky. As their spray subsided, a dark shadow came floating to the surface: the U-boat. She lay defenceless. Haysom kicked the Swordfish sideways and fell on to her again; this time for the kill. But half-way through his dive a mass of cumulus rolled ponderously across the moon; cloud shadows darkened the sea; the U-boat disappeared.

Cursing, Haysom pulled out of the dive. They would have to drop flares. It took the Swordfish several minutes to claw her way upwind to three hundred feet; and by the time Tregoning had tipped out the flares and the U-boat again stood out clearly, she was a very different target to the helpless vessel tossed up a few minutes before. For now she lay on an even keel; her gun crew were on deck; her defences were manned; a burst of tracer came flicking up at the plane.

If Haysom had stopped to think, if he hadn't been obsessed with the fear that Tregoning might think him a coward, he would have realized there was no need for him to attack the U-boat a second time—for already the destroyer, sweeping down on her fast, was less than a mile away. But he didn't think of this. He had one thought only: to attack and get it over.

'I'm going in,' he shouted, 'to finish her off.'

He flung the Swordfish seaward—straight into a curtain of fire. A stream of explosive bullets ripped into their wing. Haysom screwed up his eyes. He heard a voice screaming, a terrible crescendo of fear—the voice he recognized as his own. A numbing sickness welled up in the back of his throat. But still the fear of being thought a coward obsessed him beyond all reason, beyond all the dictates of commonsense. His eyes half-shut, his hands frozen on to the controls, he held the shattered plane on course.

The tracer hit them again. One burst smacked into the engine, another shredded their damaged wing. Flames began to pour out, like a river of molten gold. Torchlike, the plane fell seaward. Her engine cut; the wind moaned softly through her shredded wings; she no longer answered her controls. But she kept on course, and through the flames Haysom saw the U-boat grow steadily larger. He squeezed his firing-button and his last two depth-charges smacked into the sea almost beside the submarine. As they exploded, the plane belly-flopped into the sea.

The U-boat was jerked out of the water like a harpooned marlin. Thrown bodily off the crest of a wave, she toppled broken-backed into the trough that followed; and there, broken and shattered, she flung up her bows and sank. There were four survivors, four of her ack-ack crew swept by the explosion off the deck; and of these, three were injured and did not live for long.

The Swordfish hit the water surprisingly lightly. Her landing-wheels had been shot away, and the under surface of her fuselage skimmed glancing along the crest of a swell. Then her tail-plane caught in a cross-wave, and she smacked down and slewed sideways-on to the sea. Her damaged wing, the one containing the dinghy, broke off and was whirled way. Her tail-plane snapped off and sank. Geysers of steam leapt out of the water as it lapped her burning engine. But her fuselage stayed afloat.

Haysom was stunned by the impact of ditching. It was a couple of minutes before he recovered consciousness; and when he realized he was still alive he wanted to weep, not with relief but with fear, fear of what he knew would lie ahead. He began instinctively to unfasten his safety harness and scramble out of the plane. Then he remembered Tregoning. He lowered himself over the side, and treading water and clinging to the fuselage worked his way aft. The plane was low in the water, low enough for him to see into the observer's cockpit. He saw Tregoning crumpled up in a pool of moonlight, his left leg folded back.

He looked at his observer. It was every man for himself now. He'd be a fool, he told himself, to bother with an injured man. He was starting to move away when Tregoning opened his eyes. At first they were glazed and expressionless, then they filled with a familiar warmth.

'Hullo Will,' Tregoning whispered.

'Hullo Bob. You badly hurt?'

Tregoning tried to hoist himself up, but his leg folded,

and he fell to the bottom of the cockpit. The Swordfish rode the waves uneasily and settled a little lower. Haysom saw his observer watching him; his eyes were trusting.

He sighed and heaved himself up and fell wet and sodden into the cockpit.

The aircraft was breaking up as he struggled to hoist Tregoning over the side. A wave came sweeping in. It rose swirling round his waist. The Swordfish settled lower; the next wave lapped his armpits; the next his neck. The wave after that closed over his head; but as it ebbed out of the cockpit it swept them with it.

Haysom felt himself bumping awkwardly along the fuselage. With one hand he grabbed the neck of Tregoning's flying suit; with the other he clung to a wing-strut. It took him five minutes to hoist his half-conscious observer on to the wing, and another five to lash him there with torn-off strips from his mae-west. Then, panting and sick with exhaustion, he clung to the wing; and as he hung there a numbing cold began to spread upward, out of his feet.

He looked at Tregoning with sudden anger. What a fool he was being. Why waste time with a man as good as dead? He decided, for the second time, to leave Tregoning.

He was working his way along the trailing edge, when with a ripping, splintering wrench the whole wing was torn from the fuselage. Disintegrating, it spun away. Haysom grabbed at the nearest section, the one Tregoning was lashed to. In a smother of foam they were swirled forward on the crest of a great wave. He felt his hands on the sea-wet fabric begin to slip; then they dropped behind the crest, and fell into calmer water. He re-tightened his grip. Coughing and choking he levered his elbows on to the makeshift raft. It was so light his weight almost overturned it. He tried to think clearly, not just to resign himself to what was happening. But only one fact pierced the darkness of his despair. Their only hope was the raft. The raft was only three feet wide. It wasn't big enough for two.

He looked at his observer again. His anger turned to hatred. It was his life or Tregoning's now. Tregoning was half-dead already. Haysom decided to tip him off the raft.

Terror by this time had made him unbalanced, made him more than a little mad. He smiled as he pushed upward on his end of the raft; Tregoning's head was tilted under the water. He went on tilting the raft at regular, quite frequent, intervals.

A cloud rolled over the moon. It was the darkest hour of the night.

He tilted the raft gently, a little at a time, as though the rocking were the work of little waves—for he didn't want Tregoning to realize what he was doing. Once or twice he heard a muffled cry; once Tregoning's feet moved in feeble protest. He smiled; they wouldn't move much longer. His smile turned to an agonized grimace as a sudden wave of cramp pulsated through his legs. He realized that soon he would be too weak to haul himself on to the raft. He redoubled his tilting.

At last he felt certain his observer must be drowned. Now to tip him off. Slowly he clawed his way round to where Tregoning's head had lain on the sodden fabric. He saw he had tried to raise his head, by wedging the mae-west beneath his chin—he was lashed too firmly down to move his body—but he hadn't altogether succeeded. His face shone in the moonlight, translucent, sea-wet and green. Haysom felt sure he was dead. He slapped his face. To his horror the eyes flickered open. Drained of their familiar warmth, they stared at him, accusingly. Tregoning tried to speak, but no words came; only a ribbon of pale-green saliva.

To Haysom, his observer's eyes were filled with condemnation; never again would they fill with a warmth he could bask in. He was revealed now for what he was: a coward: a coward and a murderer. The will-to-live ebbed slowly out of him. His grip on the fabric loosened, and he drifted away into the arctic sea.

After a little while he turned on to his back. Looking up he saw the stars. They seemed unbearably remote. It occurred to him that he had much in common with them.

They too were cold; cold and unpitying; cold and unpitying and dead.

For some time Tregoning drifted on alone, his raft dipping erratically among the waves. Lost in a haze of pain and sickness and cold, he lay uncaring on the borderline of life and death.

Then strange things began to happen to him, things that distressed him because he could not understand them. A strange face, square and bearded, rose out of the sea; strange hands squeezed him between the shoulder-blades; and a strange voice shouted at him hoarsely in a language he did not understand. He was too tired to try and puzzle it out. For a while he was conscious of the raft being held and guided among the waves, then he lapsed into unconsciousness.

Suddenly a great light flooded over him. He opened his eyes and saw that the water had turned to gold. He wondered if he was dead. He listened and heard a dull rhythmic throbbing, like the engines of a ship. Then a wall of darkness moved towards him, blotting out the stars. He heard a confused sound of shouting. Beside him a rope smacked into the sea. The strange hands passed the rope under his armpits; then, twisting and bumping against the body of another man, he was hoisted out of the water, drawn up the curve of a hull and tipped on to a deck.

He realized that he wasn't, after all, going to die.

Someone with gentle hands cut away his flying suit; and the prick of a needle toppled him headlong into a tunnel of twisting darkness.

It was two days later that he woke and found he was in a bunk; the bunk of the master of the *San Antonio*.

Later—a long time later—he felt he ought to write to Haysom's father; and this was the most difficult letter he ever had to sit down to.

. . . *No one will ever know*, he wrote, *exactly what happened. But of one thing I'm certain. Will saved my life. I remember his hauling me out of the plane. I remember his tying me on to the raft.*

He didn't get on himself, instead he hung on to the edge of it. We stayed together for a long time, but in the end he must have dropped off with exhaustion, or perhaps with cramp . . . then this German, the only survivor from the U-boat, saw the raft and swam across to it, and we were together when the San Antonio *came back and picked us up. . . .*

And if there were certain things about that night which Tregoning did not understand, and if he had any suspicions or any doubts, he kept them strictly to himself.

.　　　.　　　.　　　.　　　.

It was still dark when the *San Antonio* rejoined the convoy. Radio silence was in force, no light could be shown; so she just edged quietly into station.

From *Viper*'s bridge Jardine watched her. She had, in the last twenty-four hours, caused him more trouble, more anxiety, than the rest of the convoy put together. But now that she was back all he had done for her seemed so very much worth while. For she was the sheep that had been lost and now was found, she was the prodigal who had come home at last. There were no flags to wave; there was no fatted calf to kill. But the joy of reunion is in the heart.

We'll be all right now, thought Jardine. Now we're together; now we are one, 'Come the three corners of the world in arms and we shall shock them . . .'

9

AT DAWN the advance screen passed the 73rd Parallel, less than a hundred and fifty miles from the edge of the pack-ice. Wind and sea had moderated a little; but the cold was sharper now, and the sun was heatless—even at noon it hugged the horizon, glowing dull red, like the embers of a dying fire, too weak to cast a shadow.

At ten o'clock two Wildcats climbed into the frozen sky; they climbed to a thousand feet, then they began to circle the convoy. They were waiting for the reconnaissance planes, which Jardine felt certain would come with the dawn. We may not be able, he thought, to stop them finding us, but at least we can make them pay. Look-outs were doubled; radar screens were conned more exactly; ack-ack crews were closed up at action stations, and hour after hour the Wildcats' vapour tracks pencilled the sky. But no planes came.

The hours passed. The brief fragment of daylight died; the convoy stood north-eastward, unmolested, apparently undiscovered. Soon it was night.

Some men were thankful, some were puzzled, others—including Jardine—were worried. For though neither plane nor U-boat had apparently come near the convoy for thirty-six hours, yet he had the feeling that they were being watched. Why he felt this, he couldn't say. But some sixth sense warned him that sea and sky were not as innocently empty as they seemed.

Soon after it was dark they crossed the 74th Parallel.

Each hour now brought them appreciably closer to Murmansk. Two days more, thought Jardine, and we'll be at the approaches to Kola Bay. He paced the bridge, wondering why they were being neither shadowed nor attacked. It wasn't, he knew, because of the weather—for that, even over Norway, had cleared. It wasn't because the Germans couldn't find the convoy—of that he felt sure, for the U-boats and the Blom and Voss must have given them a pointer too obvious to be missed. And he couldn't believe that they were giving up, were letting him through unopposed. There was in fact only one possible explanation: they wanted him to go on, they were leading him into a trap. And it was a trap there could be no avoiding: for Kola Bay could be approached only one way—down a narrow strait of water between the pack ice and the north Norwegian shore. Through this strait he would have to pass; there the trap would be set; he would somehow have to avoid it after it was sprung.

Below him, on *Viper's* flight deck, he saw his son walk slowly aft to the batting platform. For thirty-six hours young Jardine had been landing the planes at frequent intervals. He was tired now, physically and mentally. He knew the S.M.O. was watching him. He took a perverse pride in putting on a great show of energy whenever his path and the doctor's crossed; but God alone knows, he thought, how long I can keep it up. The last forty planes had touched down safely; but this, he knew, was something that couldn't go on for ever.

Viper swung into wind. He picked up his bats; he held them steady, and the forty-first plane began its approach.

At night a batsman can't see the plane he is guiding in. He can see only its lights. There are three of these; a blue navigation light on the tip of either wing, and a white 'attitude' light on the tail. According to the position of these lights, the batsman makes his signals—the navigation lights tell him the plane's height, whether she is level and whether she is in alignment with the flight deck; the 'attitude' light gives him an indication of the plane's speed, and tells him whether she is in the correct 'three-point' attitude for touching down.

As soon as the forty-first Swordfish levelled up, young Jardine saw she was coming in too fast; he signalled her to lose speed; he waited for her tail to drop, for her 'attitude' light to sink below the fuselage and into his line of vision. But no light came. Angrily he signalled her again—he had no patience with pilots who were slow to obey him. But still no light appeared. Then he noticed something else; something that nine batsmen out of ten would have missed. It was because Jardine was a good batsman, and because for each landing he keyed himself up to a state of extra-sensitive awareness, that he now noticed there was something odd about the approaching Swordfish: her navigation lights were ever so slightly shuddering, as if her wing-tips were a-tremble. He realized suddenly that in spite of the non-appearance of her tail light, she wasn't coming in too fast; she was coming in too slowly. She was about to stall; about to plummet into the sea. Frantically he signalled her to increase speed, to rise away from the deck. He heard her engine open up; saw her navigation lights rise skyward. He felt a surge of thankfulness. As he lowered his bats he was trembling. If I'd gone on signalling her to slow down, he thought, I'd have dropped her straight into the sea.

He looked up at the Swordfish as she passed high over the flight deck. As he'd expected, there was still no sign of her tail light; either the bulb had gone or the electrical circuit had failed.

He realized he had no way now of assessing her attitude or speed. Landing her would not be easy. But at least he knew what he was faced with. He spoke to Halsey and a minute later an Aldis lamp was flashing at the plane.

Then came the bustle and tension of an emergency landing: the blare of the tannoys; the clearing of catwalks; the coming on deck of the asbestos-coated fire-fighters; the silence, as the plane came drifting in.

With the pilot's eyes shifting from young Jardine's bats to his own air-speed indicator, the first approach was ragged and abortive. Half-way through the second, *Viper* began to corkscrew, and again Jardine had to wave the Swordfish away. But I don't care, he thought, if this goes on all night; sooner or later he'll manage better than this. The fourth attempt was less erratic, and *Viper* was steady on course. As the plane came low over the round-down he gave it the signal to cut.

Only one man saw what happened next.

'The signal for a pilot to cut his engine,' says the Batsman's Manual of Instruction, 'consists of the lowering and crossing of the arms. It is customary for a batsman to accompany this signal with a half step forward, at the same time ducking beneath the wingtip of the approaching plane.'

Jardine lowered and crossed his arms. He took a half step forward. He ducked. Then he realized that the plane was drifting sideways, was landing almost on top of him. It was too late to try and correct her. He flung himself to the deck. He felt a strange blast of air, warm and sickly sweet; then the plane was past. Down the length of the port catwalk men fell flat on their faces as the Swordfish came side-slipping towards them. Then, on the very edge of the flight deck, her arrestor-hook caught; her wingtip missed the bofors and oerlikons by inches; the self-centralizing wires pulled her back to the middle of the deck, and she came to a juddering halt.

There was quite a 'to-do' afterwards, with official conferences, at which Halsey, young Jardine and the Swordfish pilot all made their reports. But apart from the fact that the plane had suddenly and inexplicably drifted to port— without warning and without apparent cause—little was learned. It was, they realized, the third time this had happened since they'd pulled out of Scapa Flow.

But later that night, when young Jardine was enjoying a meal in the quiet of his cabin, someone knocked at the door. It was the Flight Deck Officer; he wanted to know what conclusion the conferences had come to.

'None,' said young Jardine, 'as far as I know.'

He went on with his meal.

'Still in the dark, eh?'

'That's right.'

'Maybe I could tell you a thing or two.'

Jardine looked at the Deck Officer curiously. He had never cared for him much.

'If you've any bright ideas,' he said, 'Wings is the man you ought to be seeing, not me.'

'I'll see him when I'm ready. Tell me, while you were batting did you notice a smell?'

'Yes; come to think of it, I did.'

'What sort of smell?'

'Hot and sickly—rather like burnt oil.'

'Before or after the plane passed you?'

'Before.'

The Deck Officer wrote carefully in a small leather pocket-book. He looked smug.

'Look here,' Jardine said, 'if you've any idea what made the plane drift over, for God's sake tell someone. It's happened three times now.'

'I'll tell someone. When I'm sure.'

'That may be too late,' said Jardine slowly, 'for some people.'

'Too bad.' The Deck Officer closed his pocket-book with a snap.

'Thanks,' he said, 'for your help. As soon as I'm ready, I'll submit my report to the Captain.'

'Take your time,' said Jardine. 'It's not your life you're playing with.'

The door shut softly. I wonder how much, thought young Jardine, he really knows?

.   .   .   .   .

While young Jardine and the Deck Officer were talking, the convoy had been rediscovered. This in itself was no surprise to Jardine, but the manner it came about confirmed his fears that they were being led into a trap.

A little after midnight four planes appeared on *Viper*'s radar screens. They headed, accurately and confidently, for the centre of the convoy—as if they already knew its whereabouts. There was no chance of avoiding them, for the night was fine and moonlit, with only a scattering of cloud. The planes closed in steadily. When they were roughly five miles from the fringe of the convoy, they climbed to varying heights and began to circle the advancing ships, just out of gun-range and with clockwork precision. Here, thought Jardine, is the start of a preconceived plan. He wondered what would happen next. Together with the First Lieutenant he paced the bridge. The throb of aircraft engines filled the sky. Occasionally a glint of moonlight silvered fuselage or wing.

'Do you think,' asked Jardine, 'they're Junkers or Blom and Vosses?'

'Junkers I'd say, sir. The B and V's engines have a heavier beat.'

Jardine nodded. He had come to the same conclusion himself.

'Notice anything else about 'em?'

The First Lieutenant shook his head.

'They're low. Unusually low for shadowing.'

They strained their eyes. Twice the First Lieutenant saw the flash of silver on a turning wing. It's true, he thought. They're not more than three thousand feet.

Jardine moved restlessly. An idea came to him; he flicked up the lid of a voice-pipe and spoke to Stone.

'What range,' he asked, 'is the Swordfish doing her patrol?'

'Fifteen miles, sir.'

'Call her up. Tell her to watch out for enemy aircraft. And,' he added, 'bring her in to five miles.'

He was about to replace the voice-pipe when another thought came to him.

'Who,' he asked, 'is the pilot?'

'The C.O., sir.'

'I thought he'd just done a patrol?'

Stone was apologetic. 'So he had,' he said. 'But as soon as he saw the aircraft on the radar screen, he asked me to let him do this one as well.'

   .   .   .   .   .

Marsden was at three hundred feet, and his Swordfish was unarmed. The Junkers were at three thousand feet, and had two forward-firing machine-guns. It was not a pleasant state of affairs. But for an hour nothing happened. Marsden, as far as possible, kept to the shadows, altering course frequently to keep beneath the patches of cloud. But there came a time when the cloud began to thin out, and between the wide-spaced patches of cumulus shone a great expanse of silver sea: without shadow, without cover. Marsden was half-way across it when he got the message from *Viper* to close in; thankfully he altered course. A few minutes later his observer called him up.

'I think,' he said, 'we're being followed.'

Marsden screwed round. Above and behind him he saw a glint of silver moving across the sky.

His observer's voice came through again.

'She's been creeping up on us the last five minutes.'

'Watch her,' Marsden said.

He banked to port and headed straight for the convoy, running for the protection of the warships' bofors and oerlikons. The plane above them also altered course. It began to close in.

Marsden saw that a little ahead was a heavy mass of cumulus; it was drifting across their path, driving a wedge of darkness between them and the convoy. He looked for the other planes; they were not to be seen. He wondered if they were waiting for him, behind the cloud. After a couple of minutes he saw a light smudge of grey break off and move upwind along the top of the cloudbank. He realized it was one of the Junkers. And seconds later he saw another, hovering beneath the cloud base. They had him cut off. Surrounded. Soon they would close in.

Three fast, well-armed monoplanes would, in daylight, have had no trouble destroying the slow, unprotected Swordfish. But Marsden had an ally now: the darkness. He looked about him, knowing his life depended on the use he made of what little cover there was.

Ahead of him was the cumulus, an unstable mass of darkness covering a couple of dozen square miles. Here, if only he could reach it, was temporary safety. He looked at the cumulus again, noting its structure. It was shaped like a crescent; its eastern tip—which was passing close to the convoy—was dark and heavy; its western tip was lighter, finer in texture and more ragged.

He began to alter course, a few degrees at a time, inching the Swordfish towards the nearest promontory of cloud; at the same time he cautiously increased height. For some minutes his manœuvres passed unnoticed. Then the Junkers above the cloud cottoned on to what was happening. It came sweeping down in a fast, purposeful dive. A second later a startled cry from Marsden's observer told him the plane behind them was attacking too, was diving on to them straight out of the moon.

They were close to the cloud now. In a couple of minutes its folds of darkness would be rolling over them. But could they last the couple of minutes?

The Junkers coming in from ahead opened fire too soon. From a thousand yards its tracer slashed at the Swordfish. Marsden swung slightly to starboard; then, as the German followed him, he cartwheeled suddenly to port. The Junkers couldn't turn as quickly as the Swordfish; the German pilot couldn't bank steeply enough to keep Marsden in his sights; his tracer, as he followed him into the turn, flashed always a fraction outside the Swordfish's canted wing. He hauled back on his stick. The planes turned more steeply; their wings swung vertical. Then the second Junkers came screaming in from the beam; her tracer slashed at the turning plane. Marsden flicked on to his back. Like a falling leaf the Swordfish toppled seaward. The Junkers followed. Between cloud and sea they wheeled and banked. Tracer ribboned the sky. The hammer of guns echoed back from the cloud. The moonlight poured down. Twice Marsden was only just in time to slideslip a vicious burst. Then, behind him, he saw the pulsating fringe of the cloud. It was mercifully near. He jerked the Swordfish round in a quivering stall turn, and the dark folds of grey came swirling over him.

Moon, sea and the attacking planes disappeared. The thud of gunfire died away. For the moment they were safe, wrapped in the enfolding veil of grey.

It was a new world they came suddenly into: a world that was silent, mysterious and darkly moving. Marsden concentrated on his instruments and climbed to the cloud centre. It was unpleasantly bumpy, with down-draughts and up-currents plucking at the plane, but at least there was no icing, and he could keep her under control. He decided to make for the westerly tip (which was farthest from the convoy); with luck, he thought, the planes will be waiting at the easterly tip, expecting us to break cover close to the ships.

Soon the cloud began to thin out. Visibility improved. Through patches of wispy grey he caught occasional glimpses of the sea. Then he broke out into open moonlit sky. The planes were nowhere to be seen.

He dropped to sea level, and began a wide detour which brought him an hour later back to the carrier.

He went at once to the bridge. There he found the First Lieutenant—Jardine and Halsey were below at a staff conference—and the Commander told him that the patrol following his had been shot down in flames.

Marsden shut his eyes. It's funny, he thought, how things work out: how we bring about the very things we try to avoid. Now, of his squadron's fifteen Swordfish only seven were left. Inexorably, plane by plane, the convoy was being stripped of its defences. By the time they came to Kola Bay, to the final testing ground, they might well, he realized, be too weak to resist the last assault.

It was this same thought that had prompted Jardine to call his staff conference—for, from the events of the last few hours, he had guessed the Germans' plan.

'They've only two days left,' he told his assembled officers. 'My guess is this. On the first day they'll try to soften us up; they'll try to exhaust us with hit-and-run attacks; they'll try to grind away our air defences. On the second day, when we're weakened and when we're so far into the narrows we can't turn back, they'll throw everything they've got into one last attack. Now these are the counter-measures I propose to take. . . .'

That night three Swordfish and two Wildcats were trundled to one side of the hangar; and Aplin, much to his surprise, was told that he had twelve hours in which to re-fuel and service them.

.   .   .   .   .

December 11th dawned fine and clear and unbelievably cold. The sea was moderate; the wind was fresh; the cloud was broken and high; and with the first glimmer of daylight came the U-boats and planes.

There were about a dozen U-boats. They came at dawn; and at sunset they were still there, worrying at the fringe of the convoy. Not once during the short arctic day did they press their attacks home. Instead they skirted the advanced screen at a discreet distance, tempting the warships and Swordfish to come after them. They would certainly have succeeded if Jardine hadn't ordered his vessels not to be drawn away. As it was, the U-boats were ignored except when they closed too dangerously; when they did this, a warship, a Swordfish and a Wildcat moved on to them in concert, pushed them back, then withdrew to safety.

The planes came not in a flood but in a continual nagging trickle; throughout the three-and-a-half hours of daylight there were always ten to twenty of them circling the convoy. They were torpedo-carrying Junkers; and like the U-boats they didn't press their attacks home; they came in singly or occasionally in pairs; they launched their torpedoes from an excessively hopeful range; then they circled the convoy waiting for the Wildcats to drive them away. If Jardine hadn't warned his pilots not to follow them, they would have fallen into the trap—and though several Junkers would have been shot down, the Wildcats too would have suffered losses. As it was the fighters spent an exhausting, unsatisfying day; hour after hour they took off, intercepted an atttack, broke it up, then came back to re-arm and refuel; they had little chance of making a definite kill, and only two Junkers were shot down. But the Wildcats did what Jardine wanted. They survived.

At noon the convoy zig-zagged past Bear Island and stood in the narrows that led to Kola Bay. And still, well into the afternoon, the attacks were kept up. They were never heavy; but they never slackened off. As soon as Jardine tried to rest his fighters, the German planes came in more boldly. As soon as he tried to withdraw his Swordfish, the U-boats approached more threateningly. He had no choice but to keep his planes in the air; to fly them to exhaustion.

In any other carrier losses would have been crippling, and by nightfall the convoy would probably have been left defenceless, shorn of its aircraft. Yet, thanks to the pilots' skill and to young Jardine's batting, the only plane lost that day was a single Wildcat which ventured too far afield, was jumped on by a pair of Junkers and shot blazing into the sea. This was at two o'clock. A few minutes later a cloud rolled over the setting sun, and the Junkers began to head for Norway.

We've been lucky, Jardine thought. The planes he had set aside in the hangar for an emergency had never been needed. He watched his son, still on the batting platform, landing the last of the Wildcats. It's due to him, he thought, more than to anyone else, that the convoy is getting through. He watched his son shading his eyes, looking into the sunset. When we left Scapa, he thought, he was only a boy; now he's turning into a man.

Soon it was dark.

With the coming of night the cold grew more intense. Little flurries of powder snow drifted down from the belts of cumulus. The water took on a frozen blue-black sheen; and in it floated little globules of ice, hard, like diamonds, broken from the edge of the pack. *Viper* altered course to the eastward, standing into the narrows between the ice-pack and the north Norwegian shore.

Once it was dark the shadowing aircraft returned. Hour after hour they circled the convoy, always a little out of range. The technical experts who monitored their trans-missions could hear them calling each other up, radioing their base, broadcasting to the U-boats now beginning to mass at the approaches to Kola Bay. The train of powder was being laid. Some time in the next thirty-six hours it would be touched off. What, Jardine wondered, would provide the match?

A little before ten that evening the Yeoman handed him a signal. The Yeoman had been bringing Jardine signals all through the evening: messages about the German planes; reports from Stone about the patrolling Swordfish; but this was a signal of a different kind. For the first time since the convoy had got under way, the Admiralty broke radio silence. Their message was brief: '*Brandenberg* and six Z class destroyers left Porsanger Fjord at 1900 hours. Their course 020°, speed 15 knots.'

10

NOWHERE in the world is there a more tempestuous battleground of wind and water than at the mouth of Porsanger Fjord. Here, on the northernmost tip of Europe, winds from the Siberian plateaux meet waves that have swept a thousand miles, unchecked, from the Greenland shore. Where they come together the air is torn into vortexes and eddies, and great whirlpools and waterspouts are sucked out of the tortured sea. Watching this eternal conflict are the Kiolen hills: silent and lifeless, snow-covered to sea level and rising sheer out of the fjord. Here, legend had it, was the home of the mythical giants of Norse folklore: the land of iron and ice: the land where no man could live.

A little way down the fjord a makeshift boom had been built to try and protect the *Brandenberg* and her destroyers from the worst of the sea. But no man-made shelter could tame the waves that rolled into Porsanger Fjord. The ships jerked and bucketed and dragged their anchors; theirs was a nightmare holding ground.

For five days they had been waiting; waiting for the storm to die and their sailing orders to come through. Now on the afternoon of December 11th the orders came at last. Late into the evening Aldis lamps flickered across the fjord, and pinnaces heavy with senior officers moved silently among the darkened ships. Soon the anchor chains were rattling inboard, and the warships in line ahead were moving quietly past the boom. They headed down the fjord. After an hour they came to the open sea. Rounding North Cape, they stood north-eastward heading for the drift ice. Here among the floes and icebergs they would wait; wait for the coming of the convoy.

Their sailing had been swift and silent, but it had not been secret. For at the mouth of Porsanger Fjord is a little hill that rises sharply above its fellows; near its crest a makeshift igloo had been cut out of the snow; and in the igloo were two Norwegian fishermen. One had died of exposure—for they had been there a long time—but the other saw the *Brandenberg* and her destroyers as they filed down the fjord. His radio set was tuned-in to the Shetlands, and within an hour his message had been relayed to the Admiralty.

The *Brandenberg* crossed Jardine's bows at a range of eighty miles. At such a distance no radar could have detected her. But Jardine, forewarned, had sent a Swordfish to patrol ahead of the convoy; and a little after midnight the plane picked up the warships on the screen of her A.S.V.X. She cut short her patrol and headed back for the carrier.

When Jardine heard the pilot's report, he was reminded of Marsden's wager, made at the start of the voyage: 'If the *Brandenberg* comes out,' the C.O. had said, 'I'll lay three to one we sink her.' That of course had been when they had a full squadron aboard. Now they had only seven planes. But remembering that a dozen Swordfish at Taranto had sunk half the Italian Fleet, Jardine called Marsden to the bridge.

. . . . .

All that night the convoy headed into the narrows. To port was the pack-ice; to starboard was the north Norwegian shore; ahead lay the *Brandenberg*, and beyond her, at the approaches to Kola Bay, the U-boats were beginning to mass. It was a night to fray the nerves.

Jardine kept two aircraft continually in the air: an A/S

patrol circling the convoy, and a shadower watching the *Brandenberg*. Two hours before dawn the shadowing aircraft reported that the German cruiser was again under way; screened by her destroyer escort, she was starting to skirt the pack-ice on a similar course to Jardine's. For a while the two fleets ran parallel. Then, quite suddenly, the *Brandenberg* swung south: she increased speed; she headed straight for the convoy.

'Action Stations!'

The blare of hooters and klaxons tumbled men out of their sleep. Look-outs were doubled, gun-directors and torpedo tubes were manned, and in every ship the radar grids swung north-eastward, probing the darkness on the convoy's bow.

By nine o'clock the *Brandenberg* was only thirty miles to the north. And she was closing fast.

So, thought Jardine, the holocaust will come with the dawn, with the pale anaemic light that round about ten o'clock will come crawling out of the east. He ordered his ships to battle stations, knowing that for the next couple of hours the fate of the convoy would hang in the balance.

One thing distressed him. Already, before the engagement had even started, he felt desperately tired; felt his perception blunted by lack of sleep, his judgment impaired by the days of anxiety and strain. From the pocket of his oilskins he took a small bottle. He swallowed two benzedrine tablets, and within ten minutes his energy and confidence came flooding back.

In his sea cabin he explained the details of his plan to a handful of senior officers. The *Brandenberg*, he said, would expect the convoy to consist of an inner core of merchantmen, ringed by a circle of warships—those were the normal dispositions. She would hope to make a surprise attack; to break through the warships and get among the merchantmen—and if she succeeded she might well annihilate the convoy in something under an hour.

'But,' Jardine said, 'she won't succeed. For her attack won't be a surprise. We've a Swordfish watching her. We'll know every move she makes. We'll know exactly where, and exactly when, she's going to strike. And we'll be waiting for her.

'All escorts I'm moving on to the northern flank. That's where she'll strike. We'll hold fire until she's committed to an attack. Then we'll halt her, cripple her and with luck sink her. If need be we'll use the last of our Swordfish to finish her off. Are there any questions?'

It was a dangerous plan; for it left the south of the convoy unprotected. Also it involved drawing the *Brandenberg* close to the merchantmen; and the *Brandenberg* was a powerful ship, with a fire power heavier than any of Jardine's (and the German Z class destroyers were large, fast and modern). If Jardine drew them on too far, if he didn't halt them at exactly the right moment, they would destroy him utterly.

Agnew asked what were their plans for disengaging, in case the *Brandenberg* broke through.

'I'm not,' said Jardine, 'making any.'

After that there were no more questions, and the conference broke up.

.   .   .   .   .

The *Brandenberg* came sweeping out of the north. The German Admiral imagined he held a trump card: the element of surprise. But the boot was on the other foot. Jardine's patrolling Swordfish reported his every move. Every few minutes the pilot's reports were passed to Jardine on *Viper*'s bridge.

'Seven warships in line abreast. Bearing 015°. Range 20 miles.'

'Seven warships in line abreast. Bearing 008°. Range 15 miles.'

Jardine's cruisers swung broadside-on, to deploy their full arcs of fire. Guns and torpedo tubes were loaded. The radar antennae swung on to their target.

The light grew pale. The range shrank. Little flurries of

snow swept over the waiting ships. A single Aldis flashed from *Viper*'s bridge. The match was dropped on the powder train.

Jardine's three cruisers opened fire at a range of 14,000 yards.

From a dozen six-inch and eight-inch turrets great banners of flame leapt into the startled sky. The clap and shudder of gunfire echoed among the clouds. Over the cruisers acrid swirls of smoke and the smell of burning cordite streamed away downwind. For half a minute there was a shocked silence. Then, a second time, the sheets of flame licked out. In their light Jardine could see the snow-flakes spinning and whirling; they were blood red. He focused his binoculars on the northern horizon. There, his first salvos were beginning to fall.

Half the guns had been loaded with starshell. High over the *Brandenberg* the sky burst suddenly to light. A galaxy of yellow balls, like spectral suns, came swinging down on the cruiser; she shuddered to a halt, bathed in their harsh, metallic glare. The outline of her turrets, bridge and fore-mast rose sharply delineated out of the whirling snow: a perfect target. Again Jardine's guns rumbled out. And now, added to the growl of the main turrets, was the sharper bark of his secondary armament: the 4.7-inch and 4-inch guns of cruisers, destroyers and corvettes.

Jardine saw that the *Brandenberg* was hit; but she seemed to be neither crippled nor halted. He saw her, in the dying light of the starshell, swing broadside-on. He heard the snarl of far-off guns as she returned his fire. Seconds later there came a thin screaming as the shells scythed high over-head. She had overestimated the range. Then, unexpec-tedly, a salvo of starshell burst over the *Atalanta*—one of the Z class destroyers had got their range exactly—and Jardine's ships, in their turn, were bathed in brilliant light.

The two fleets swung parallel. Seven miles apart, their guns trumpeted out.

The convoy came under heavy fire.

Shell splashes straddled the *Atalanta*. A near miss buckled the bow of a corvette. One of the merchantmen was hit

157

amidships; beside her funnel a fire began to glow, in dark uneven spurts. Then *Viper* was straddled by the *Brandenberg*. On either side of the carrier great columns of water rose steeple high, as the cruiser's eight-inch shells heaved up the sea. High over her flight deck the columns towered, like phantoms draped in transparent veils of spray; for a couple of seconds they hung poised in mid-air; then with a roar like a collapsing house, they fell. Great cataracts of water swept the carrier's deck. Shell-splinters knifed like molten needles into her hull. The crews of her starboard oerlikons were shredded to pulp.

The convoy reeled under the hail of fire. But the shells that rained on Jardine's ships were nothing to the hammer-blows that pulverized the Germans.

In the opening minutes of the action the *Brandenberg* was straddled six times and hit four times. She veered off course, belching smoke. Then she turned away.

Jardine guessed she was crippled. He shifted his fire to the destroyers.

Two eight-inch shells from the *Atalanta* slammed into the boiler-room of the flotilla leader. She slewed off course. She lost way. A blast of scalding steam tore open her fore-deck; and through the noise of tearing metal her crew heard the hiss of water flooding into her engines. They were beginning to abandon ship, when another shell landed flush on the bridge. The destroyer's fire-walls collapsed. A blast of hot air swept into her ammunition locker; and with a terrible internal explosion she broke her back and sank in a vortex of oil and wreckage and broken bodies, sucked down together as she dropped a thousand fathoms to the bed of the arctic sea.

Three more destroyers were hit in those first few minutes. Two suffered only minor damage, and managed to limp away; but the third was hit close to her waterline. Her speed dropped. She was hit again. She was set on fire. The fire spread. It gave Jardine's gun-layers a point to aim at, and soon a torrent of fire was raining on to the helpless ship. Hit after hit crashed into her. Heavy explosions tore her internally. She began to rock and tremble. A slow shuddering vibration loosened the plates of her hull. She was beaten low into the water. Splinters hammered like hail into her superstructure; and round her the salvoes that fell wide tore open the sea, heaving great floods of water over her listing deck. At last she turned slowly on her side. Oil spread over the sea. For a little while she stayed afloat, her propellers revolving spasmodically; then the long waves closed over her.

The German Admiral's first reaction had been to stay and fight it out; to break through the warships, and get at the convoy which he knew lay beyond. But he quickly realized that the ships opposing him were too strong; he had run into more than he'd bargained for; he was not the trapper, but the trapped. He gave the signal to disengage.

One of his leading destroyers increased speed. Pulling out of line she cut across the bow of the convoy, making smoke. Soon a pall of darkness was screening the disengaging ships. Seeing the smoke Jardine realized that the *Brandenberg* was trying to escape; he knew that—damaged though she was—unless he acted quickly she would get away. He sent in four of his destroyers.

They attacked in two pairs. *Juno* and *Jaguar* went straight through the smoke-screen; *Dauntless* and *Defiant* set off on a detour, planning to attack from an unexpected quarter, while the *Brandenberg* was engaging the first pair.

The German cruiser picked up *Juno* and *Jaguar* on her radar while they were still in the smoke-screen. At a range of ten thousand yards she opened fire. The destroyers were hopelessly out-gunned but they closed in. As they came out of the smoke, starshell broke the sky above them, flooding them in a light far brighter than a tropic noon. Then came the scream and hiss of heavy shells as the *Brandenberg*'s eight-inch salvos thudded into the sea.

Jaguar was hit; hit badly. Her for'ard turret was buckled and had to be flooded; her oerlikon and pompoms were flung shattered across her fore-deck; she lost speed. Then an eight-inch shell landed flush on her stern. She came to a shuddering halt. She had just enough way on her to swing broadside on and fire her torpedoes, but no hits were observed.

A little behind her, *Juno* kept on course, miraculously unscathed. She closed rapidly: 9,000 yards, 7,000, 5,000. The sea around her kept heaving skyward; splinters scythed through her bridge; a German destroyer launched eight torpedoes at her, which she combed as if on manœuvres in the Clyde, and soon she could see the *Brandenberg*, could see not only the flash of her guns, but the great ship herself. With the range down to 3,000 yards, *Juno* spun broadside on. She launched her torpedoes; then she fled.

The torpedoes were well aimed, but at the very moment they thudded into the sea the *Brandenberg* turned—she had spotted *Dauntless* and *Defiant* coming in across her bow. The torpedoes snaked harmlessly behind her.

But *Juno*'s attack had served its purpose. The *Brandenberg* had been engaging her so fiercely, she had failed to notice the second pair of destroyers until it was too late.

Two explosions, long and deeply echoing, blanketed off the thud and clatter of gunfire. The sea stirred uneasily. The gunfire died away. There was a moment of silence; then *Dauntless* fired a salvo of starshell. Six dazzling balls of yellow-white soared high into the air, lighting the crippled cruiser in a pitiless, metallic glare, exposing the dark, still-smoking caverns where the torpedoes had exploded on her waterline. The *Brandenberg* had flung up her helm. Now, listing drunkenly, she fell away, wreathed in smoke and steam and the fumes of burning cordite.

Their work done, the destroyers withdrew.

They left behind them a ship that was crippled, but was far from defenceless. A ship that now turned like a wounded tiger at bay.

As the destroyers withdrew, the *Brandenberg* was left alone. In the momentary lull her crew worked desperately. Used cartridge shells were salvaged; the heavy turrets were turned briefly into wind (for the cordite gases to be blown away); munition hoists and racks were restocked; below, watertight partitions were strengthened, damage was hastily repaired; and the engines were coaxed into reluctant life.

Their breathing space was longer than the German Admiral had dared to hope for. Soon the *Brandenberg* was again under way.

Slowly and painfully, at a meagre couple of knots, she began to limp away from the convoy. She expected, any moment, to pick up the British destroyers, coming in for the kill. But the minutes passed, and no destroyers came.

For Jardine could spare neither ships nor aircraft to finish her off. That was the tragedy: that he had the *Brandenberg* at his mercy—crippled, shorn of her escort, cut off from her base—yet he couldn't finish what he had begun. For in the south, on the convoy's unprotected flank, his Swordfish had reported a U-boat pack was moving in; and he knew he would need every plane and every warship to keep this new danger at bay. In twos and threes his destroyers and corvettes were withdrawn; his Swordfish were vectored south, and soon the *Brandenberg* was alone. Watched by a solitary destroyer that shadowed her by radar she went limping away to the north-west.

.   .   .   .   .

The U-boats had hoped to find the convoy scattered. But instead of a mêlée of frightened ships, driven southward by the *Brandenberg*, they met an alert, well-organized defence: a pair of patrolling Swordfish and a screen of destroyers and corvettes. Something had gone wrong. Their attacks became unco-ordinated; half-hearted; easily repulsed. As soon as they found the convoy guarded, the majority of them submerged and set course for Kola Bay.

.   .   .   .   .

Behind the screen of warships, Jardine's merchantmen searched for survivors from the German destroyers. But of five hundred men, only thirty were saved. Two, more dead than alive, were hauled aboard the carrier. Their eyes swollen and sightless, their faces encrusted with frost and salt and oil, they were pitiable remnants of men. But they were the lucky ones. Their companions died terribly; died of cold, exhaustion and exposure, their lifeblood quickly congealing in the cruel arctic sea.

When the last of the survivors had been picked up the convoy again got under way. The ships that were damaged limped into the convoy centre. Speed was reduced to four knots to enable *Jaguar* and the damaged merchantmen to keep station. And within three hours of the start of the action, Jardine's vessels were again heading for Kola Bay.

Was this, he wondered, the victory he had dreamed of? Was the way to Murmansk open at last? It could be. For now, with every hour, they were moving into waters that came increasingly under Russian control. Tomorrow morning Russian planes would be giving them air cover; tomorrow afternoon Russian patrol boats would be leading them into the Bay. If no other attacks developed that afternoon, they were as good as home.

But what of the *Brandenberg*? He was torn between duty and desire; between his obligation to protect the convoy, and his eagerness to give the cruiser the *coup de grâce*. He decided reluctantly that he couldn't spare the warships to hunt her down—that would be weakening the convoy too dangerously. Nor could he risk his few remaining planes in a daylight torpedo attack—when losses would inevitably be heavy. He would have to wait until it was dark; then, if the *Brandenberg* was still within range, his Swordfish would stand a better chance.

The convoy moved steadily eastward.

A few minutes before sunset Jardine went into the chartroom to check the *Brandenberg*'s position. She was fifty miles to the west heading for home, for the shelter of Porsanger Fjord. His planes, if they went after her now, would be operating at longish range; losses would be inevitable. He sighed, and called Marsden to the bridge.

.   .   .   .   .

On the after end of the flight deck three planes were ranged for take-off. The engines were warming up. The pilots, Marsden, Saunders and Ellis (the senior Swordfish pilot), were strapping themselves in. Jardine, as he watched them preparing for take-off, thought what a pitiably small striking force they were to attack a powerful, heavily defended cruiser; but they were all he could spare.

Viper swung into wind. An Aldis flashed from the bridge. Marsden revved up his engine till the Swordfish hung quivering against her brakes; then he released her. Slowly gathering speed, the plane, weighed down by her 21-inch torpedo, went lumbering down the flight deck. She sank over the bows, almost feathered the sea, then climbed awkwardly away.

Looking back, Marsden saw two blue navigation lights creeping slowly towards him. Soon the lights took up station, one on either side; he knew then that the other planes were with him, flying in close formation. It was too dark for him to see their silhouettes. He climbed to a thousand feet then headed westward, towards the last-reported position of the *Brandenberg*.

Their A.S.V.X. soon picked the cruiser up at a range of forty miles. For a while Marsden kept at a thousand feet, while the observers worked out the *Brandenberg*'s bearing, course and speed; then he took the formation down to sea-level, to avoid detection by the German radar. Close to the still invisible waves they flew on. After a few minutes a golden crescent swung out of the southern sea: the rising moon.

At sea-level the A.S.V.X. was less effective; and on the observers' screens the image of the *Brandenberg* faded gradually away. But by this time they had a bearing on her. They kept on course. And after half an hour her image reappeared: almost dead ahead, at a range of fifteen miles. The planes drew together. They sank even closer to the sea. The pilots checked their switches. Soon the *Brandenberg* was very near.

Marsden switched off his navigation lights. The planes broke formation. They swept in to the attack.

Saunders broke away to port. Skirting the *Brandenberg* he manœuvred himself upwind of her. Then he began to climb. Slowly the needle crept round the dial of his altimeter: 500 feet, 1,500, 3,000. Soon he was in position to drop his flares, two miles upwind of the still silent cruiser. He looked at his watch; another thirty seconds and the other planes would be ready.

Soundlessly, a thin line of sighting tracer came swimming out of the sea. It was well aimed. There was a splitting explosion, an acrid smell of cordite, and the Swordfish toppled seaward. Three of the *Brandenberg*'s searchlights leapt into the sky, their questing fingers following the tracer. Hungrily they swept from side to side, cutting great swathes of light out of the sky. As Saunders pulled the Swordfish level one of them caught him. A cold, metallic light flooded over the plane, throwing the outline of wings and struts into sharp relief. Saunders was blinded. Before he could take avoiding action, the other searchlights came sweeping on to him, intersecting him, pinpointing him on a tripod of dazzling light. Then came the ack-ack: salvos from three dozen guns tearing open the sky. The Swordfish jerked, trembled and staggered.

'The flares!' Saunders shouted. 'Quick. Before we're hit.'

He held the plane level while the sky around them was split by vortexing explosions. Shrapnel the size of cricket balls crashed into their fuselage; the engine screamed in protest; the plane rocked; Saunders needed all his strength to hold her on course, while his observer tipped out the flares. Burning fiercely the arcs of light swung down on the *Brandenberg*—like fireships drifting in with a flood tide. Not until the last flare had been released did Saunders slip out of the searchlights; then he dropped to sea-level, and checked the damage to his plane.

Waiting to launch his attack, Marsden saw the flares come swinging over the *Brandenberg*. Bathed in a lurid blood-red glow, the cruiser turned at bay, smoke and cordite fumes streaming away downwind. Flames from her ack-ack pulsated out. Even as Marsden watched, two of the flares were hit and knocked spinning into the sea. The light about the *Brandenberg* grew fainter.

Marsden dived in steeply. He was within a mile of the cruiser before she spotted him; then as he passed out of darkness and into the light of the flares the cruiser's ack-ack thudded out. He swung the Swordfish sharply from side to side; then, crossing his controls, sent her slithering seaward in a breath-catching sideslip. But the fire was too heavy for him to avoid it all. The Swordfish shuddered as a salvo burst beneath her wingtip; she was thrown half on to her back; shrapnel beat like hail into the belly of her fuselage. By the time Marsden had righted her, the *Brandenberg* was very near. He pulled out of his dive thirty feet from the sea. His torpedo dropped. He flung the plane aside and fled zig-zagging out of the flare light. As darkness closed merci-fully round him, the ack-ack died away.

For a long moment there was silence. I've missed her, Marsden thought. But how could I, at a range like that? He banked the plane round and waited; the seconds seemed like hours; then came a long, reverberating roar.

The torpedo hit the *Brandenberg* amidships, less than a dozen feet from where, five hours earlier, she had been hit by *Dauntless*. A thin pyramid of flame leapt skyward. The cruiser shuddered to a stop. An angry glow lit up the holo-caust between her decks, where her watertight doors had collapsed and the sea swept into her engine room. Listing drunkenly, she began to yaw out of control among the wide-spaced waves.

But her guns still thudded out; and Ellis, attacking from astern, ran into heavy fire. He dived in steeply, with a minimum of avoiding action, trying to force a way through the curtain of flak. But in his determination to align his sights accurately, he spent too long on the same course. The gunners got his range. A stream of bullets ripped into his wing; a shell struck him flush in the engine; and, disin-tegrating, the Swordfish fell seaward. Ellis slumped forward;

his finger clamped on to the release button; his torpedo shot clear; but it hit the water steeply, and sank. And the Swordfish, when it hit the sea, sank as quickly and noiselessly as the torpedo.

Saunders attacked last. All the flares but two had been shot out now; and the *Brandenberg* lay bathed in a softer, less garish, light. Downwind of the crippled ship streamed smoke and cordite fumes, and through these Saunders came in low, hidden by the acrid clouds and guided by the glow of the fires now raging in the *Brandenberg*. He was almost on top of her before he was spotted. The flak was hurried and inaccurate. He took his time aligning his sights; then his torpedo thudded into the sea; and it ran true.

It hit the *Brandenberg* in her most vulnerable spot: about ten feet in front of her screws. Her stern was blown entirely away. A wall of sea water crashed on to her already listing deck, and the great ship fell away. With the waves pounding into her, she was beaten lower and lower into the water. Then, very slowly, she turned on to her side.

She lay there for several minutes, wreathed in steam, torn by internal explosions. Her searchlights, still switched on, glowed chalk-white under the water. A film of oil spread thickly round her. Suddenly her stern reared skyward. A great whirlpool was torn out of the sea, and into this the *Brandenberg* was slowly drawn. Quietly she spiralled down, like a falling leaf on a still October morning, to the bottom of the sea.

The night returned to silence and to darkness.

Marsden flew low over the place where the *Brandenberg* had been. He dropped flare-markers; and they lit up the handful of men clinging to pieces of wreckage. Tentatively one of the German destroyers—which had been brought back by the sound of gunfire—switched on her searchlight. Its narrow finger of white swept over the survivors. The destroyer moved in to pick them up.

For a while Marsden and Saunders watched. Then they set course for the rendezvous where they had agreed to meet: ten miles east of where the *Brandenberg* had been

attacked. Here they hoped to form up and fly in formation back to the carrier.

Saunders reached the rendezvous first. For a while he circled round, but there was no sign of the other planes. The night was dark. His Swordfish was damaged. With every minute *Viper* was drawing farther away. He wondered how long he could afford to wait. After ten minutes he fired a salvo of starshell, hoping Marsden or Ellis would see it and close with him. But no planes came. He wondered if he was the only one to come out of the attack alive; or perhaps he was circling the wrong position? At last he decided he could wait no longer. He set course for the carrier, alone.

After dropping his flare-markers Marsden too set course for the rendezvous. His plane was also damaged; and among other things his gyro-compass had been shattered, and he had to rely on his observer to keep him on course by calling out readings from the compass in the rear cockpit. Neither Marsden nor his observer knew that lodged in the Swordfish fuselage, within a few inches of this compass, was a splinter of shrapnel: highly magnetic. The compass was reading 70° off-true.

So in due course Marsden found himself circling a position which he thought was the rendezvous, but which was in fact well to the south-westward of where they had agreed to meet. He waited there a long time, and when no other planes appeared, he too set out for the carrier. But his course was not—as he thought—easterly towards the *Viper*, but southerly; towards the Norwegian shore.

.   .   .   .

Young Jardine paced the flight deck. Radio silence was in force, so he had no news of how the attack had gone or when the planes would be back. The strain of the last few days was catching up with him now. Since the dying-out of the storm he had landed close on a hundred aircraft; some of them had landed in snow-squalls, most of them had landed at night, all of them had landed when the carrier was pitching steeply. The only mishaps to date had been a couple of broken tail-skids, and one Swordfish rolling gently into the barrier; but all the time the strain and the tension and the lack of sleep had been building up to a climax. And now the climax was at hand. Young Jardine knew that if only he could land the striking force safely the end of his responsibilities would be in sight—for tomorrow they would be within the orbit of Russian shore-based planes; tomorrow there'd be little if any flying. Now he waited tensely, keyed-up; listening for the engine beat of the returning Swordfish.

He waited a long time. The minutes seemed like hours, the hours like aeons. Then softly through the falling snow came the throb of a Pegasus engine. The tannoy clicked on. His father's voice, quiet and emotionless, filled the ship:

'Stand by to land-on one Swordfish.'

My God, young Jardine thought, only one.

She came low over *Viper*'s bows, her Aldis flashing. Almost at once the telephone by the batting platform began to whirr. Young Jardine picked it up.

'Bats speaking.'

'Halsey here, Bats. I'm afraid she's damaged.'

'Badly?'

'The pilot thinks not. But you'd like the searchlight on her, I expect?'

'Please.'

Three times the Swordfish flew low over the flight deck, winging moth-like along the beams of the searchlights. In their chalk-white light young Jardine saw the shredded wingtip and the shattered undercarriage. He shivered. He decided to try to land her well forward, to make her crash into the barrier before her broken landing-gear slewed her over the side. He picked up his bats.

He wondered who the pilot was: Marsden, Ellis or Saunders? He remembered Marsden's kindness to him, the way he had taken him under his wing, and thinking of the shredded wingtip and the shattered undercarriage hoped that the plane wasn't his. As soon as it began its approach,

169

his anxiety on this point was relieved; for the C.O. invariably landed off a turn; this pilot used an approach that was long and straight. He guessed it was Saunders.

The snow eased up a little as the Swordfish came drifting in. Saunders realized he was being brought in high; several times he tried to throttle back and sink, but always Jardine motioned him up. And he had the good sense to obey. On his third attempt, the carrier's deck rose obligingly at the right moment. Jardine gave him the signal to cut, and the plane dropped vertically, from twenty feet, flush on the last arrestor wire. She dropped heavily but squarely. Her undercarriage snapped cleanly off. She started to slew towards the catwalk; but before she reached it she hit the barrier. Her propeller, flaying into the steel meshes, held her fast; and Saunders and his observer scrambled out, unhurt.

The news spread quickly: the *Brandenberg* had been sunk; but elation was tinged with apprehension. What of the rest of their planes? What of their C.O.? The carrier settled down to wait.

Young Jardine sat huddled on the edge of his batting platform. He wanted to be ready the moment they came in sight. At first he felt certain they would come. He told himself that he would have known intuitively if anything had happened to Marsden. But gradually his certainty gave way to doubt. And after doubt, came fear. The snow fell softly; the waves sighed along *Viper*'s bow; the minutes lengthened into hours; and still the sky was silent and the radar screens were blank. At last young Jardine realized that the planes had been gone a full five hours. He knew then, with terrible certainty, that Marsden could never return.

The night seemed suddenly colder, the darkness more intense. Walking down the flight deck, young Jardine shivered. It was cold on the carrier; it would be colder still in the sea. The cold spread from his body into his heart. He looked at the sky and saw a single star swing gem-like through a rift in the cloud. You weren't hung there, he thought, by God. There's no God. Silhouetted above the bridge rail he saw his father's head and shoulders, outlined darkly against the sky. How can you stand there, he thought, doing nothing, saying nothing, feeling nothing? Isn't there a drop of pity in you? He covered his face with his hands; and the tears ran warmly between his fingers.

He felt a hand on his shoulder, and turning saw the S.M.O. The doctor took him below.

Later, when they were sitting in the wardroom, the doctor said quietly:

'I know it sounds trite; but you'll forget all this in time.'

Young Jardine shivered. You're wrong, he thought, some things are never forgotten.

.   .   .   .   .

It was half an hour after he had made his attack that Marsden began to suspect their compass. It was not to begin with a suspicion he could attach much importance to; only an ill-defined feeling that things were not quite as they should be. Then the moon appeared through a rift in the cloud. He had been expecting it on their quarter, but now it swung into view almost dead ahead. There was no way of checking the compass. They could only fly on.

They had been airborne about two hours when Marsden's observer picked up a strange echo on his A.S.V.X., an echo that spread over nearly half the screen. It certainly wasn't the convoy. He studied it with growing dismay, for it looked like the shadow of a distant shore. As they approached the echo, and it gained in definition, his fears were confirmed. He realized then that they were hopelessly lost

Soon, over the rim of his engine cowling, Marsden could see the curve of the coastline, standing out sharply dead ahead and fading away to darkness on either flank.

It was a shore of utter desolation that they came to twenty minutes later: great waves hammering at iron cliffs, and solidifying instantly into a fringe of ice. Inland they saw the tundra, mile after mile of virgin snow; and beyond it the dark sweep of the coniferous forests. It was a lunar landscape; a world with neither colour, movement, nor life. Marsden realized that even if he managed to crash-land they wouldn't live for long in such a wilderness as this.

They turned to the left (eastward they hoped) and flew parallel to the shore, trying to pinpoint their position. The coastline had a depressing similarity. After a little while they came to a low peninsula. Beyond it the shore fell away to the south and they crossed the mouth of a fjord. On the further side of the fjord was a rugged promontory, tipped with a lone, ice-fluted mountain. As soon as he saw the mountain Marsden's observer pinpointed their position: they were on the north-westerly tip of the Baranger Penin-sula. They were able now to calculate the deviation of their compass; to work out their bearing from the convoy. Marsden's observer worked quickly—knowing that with every second their petrol was draining away—and almost at once he saw that they wouldn't have enough petrol to get them back.

They weighed up their chances, and headed out to sea, knowing that somewhere between ships and shore they would have to ditch. They knew they had only one slender chance of survival—that Jardine would spot them ap-proaching on his radar, would see them disappear and would send back a ship to pick them up. It seemed a for-lorn hope; a thousand-to-one chance; but even that was better than the certainty of freezing to death in the tundra.

They reckoned their petrol would last for another half-hour—enough for them to cover some fifty to fifty-five miles. And the convoy was ninety miles to the north. Marsden climbed slowly to three thousand feet—the higher they were the better the chances of Jardine's radar picking them up. When he had done this he could only fly on, coaxing the last possible mile out of his already damaged engine. Behind them the coastline gradually faded. Ahead, the sea gleamed silver in the moonlight: silver and empty. They felt very much alone.

But after twenty-five minutes a faint smudge darkened

the screen of their A.S.V.X. At first they hardly dared to hope; but gradually, as the echo gained in clarity, they became increasingly sure it was the convoy. They had just worked out its range—thirty-five miles—when their engine cut: cut stone dead.

.   .   .   .   .

Leading Seaman Forde yawned. Radar duty bored him. He'd better things to do, he told himself, than watch a great empty screen that danced and flickered like the panel of one of them queer new-fangled television sets; especially when any fool could tell that the screen would be blank for hours (weren't they out of Jerry's range; and the Russians never flew at night . . . had too much sense). He doodled absent-mindedly on his signal pad, adding the First Lieutenant's head to the torso of his favourite film star. He rather fancied himself as an artist. His attention shifted gradually from screen to signal pad. The number of drawings increased. An occasional glance, he told himself, was all the screen needed.

It was during one such glance that he noticed the faintest sliver of a shadow on the very edge of the screen. He told himself it was atmospheric distortion. He went on sketching the Old Man's head on top of Rita Hayworth. When he had finished, he took another look at the screen; he studied the shadow this way and that; doubtfully he tapped his teeth with his pencil. At last he got up, slid open the door of the Ops Room and told Stone he thought he'd picked up an echo, range forty miles.

Stone was busy with his U-boat plot.

'You *think* you've got an echo?' he said.

'I'm not sure, sir. It's so faint.'

Stone grunted.

'I'll come and look in a second,' he said, and went on adding to the U-boat plot. By the time he came across to the screen the echo had disappeared.

Forde sucked his teeth disconsolately.

'It was there a minute ago,' he said.

'Where?'

Forde, by instinct, had jotted down the echo's range and bearing on his signal pad. To check his figures, he picked the pad up. Stone saw the drawings.

'Very pretty,' he said. 'Now come along with me. And,' he added, 'bring your pad with you.'

Forde, breathing heavily, picked up the pad.

'It could only have been on the screen a few seconds, sir,' he grumbled.

'You'd better save your explanations,' said Stone, 'for the Captain.'

Forde followed him on to the bridge. For some time he couldn't understand what all the fuss was about; couldn't see why the Old Man was questioning him so minutely as to exactly what the echo had looked like and exactly where it had disappeared. It was a chance remark of the First Lieutenant that gave him the clue.

'If he *had* hit the coast,' Agnew said, 'and then headed back, that's just about where he'd have got to.'

Forde realized then that the echo he had looked at so casually might have been one of their Swordfish. But it was no good wishing now that he'd noted it more carefully.

When Jardine had extracted the last fragment of information out of Forde, he paced the bridge. Had the plane been one of theirs? The odds were, he decided, that it had— what other plane would approach from the north Norwegian shore and then unaccountably vanish? But what could he do about it? To the south lay the U-boats, and possibly the remnants of the Z class destroyers limping back for Porsanger Fjord. Once before he had surrendered to sentiment and had turned the convoy back. He had got away with it then, but he had sworn never again. And never again it would be. Perhaps he could send a warship back? Yet it seemed utterly out of proportion to risk a ship, and a hundred and fifty men, on the slender chance of picking up two survivors who might or might not be alive by the time they were found. He tried to harden his heart.

He walked across to the bridge rail and stood motionless, staring out to sea. He saw his son come slowly across the flight deck; saw him cover his face with his hands; saw the S.M.O. take him below. The things, he thought, this convoy is doing to us.

On the bridge he felt confined; boxed-in. He climbed down a companionway, and began to walk up and down the flight deck. It was still only ten minutes since the plane had disappeared from the radar screen; if he wanted to search for it there was still time. His heart implored him to send back a destroyer; his brain warned him that the risk was out of all proportion. He walked on, hardly noticing where he was going. Then, acting on impulse, he went below: down to the hangar. Soon he was looking down into the heart of the carrier.

The heart was beating feebly.

A week ago the hangar had been a place of noise and bustle and twenty-three close-packed planes. Now it was silent; silent and near-deserted. Three Wildcats were secured in a far corner; two Swordfish, fuelled and armed, waited beside the lift. The rest of the planes had gone; and they would not come back. The maintenance crews were below—there were no planes left for them to maintain— only a skeleton watch, some dozen ratings, moved aimlessly about, like the caretakers of a long-deserted house. For several minutes Jardine stood motionless; his heart was thudding too quickly; his brain was a box imprisoning a fluttering bird. Then he turned away. He stumbled back to the bridge. He called for the Yeoman of Signals. He gave him detailed search instructions to send to one of the destroyers. He watched as a couple of minutes later *Dauntless* pulled away to the south. God forgive me, he thought, if anything happens to her.

.   .   .   .   .

The engine cut: cut stone dead. Marsden eased the Swordfish into a shallow dive, and they drifted down; the wind sighed through their struts; the sea rose up to meet them. At two hundred feet he turned into wind and tried to ditch diagonally, along the crest of a swell; but as he levelled off the wave-crest dropped away and left them stalling, thirty feet above the sea. Vertically the Swordfish plummeted down.

There was a tearing impact; a wall of water came crashing into the cockpits, and almost at once the Swordfish began to sink. They had less than a minute in which to undo their safety-belts, scramble on to the wing and release their dinghy. They did it with a couple of seconds to spare. Then the plane went down. As they tumbled into the half-inflated dinghy, the rope securing it to the wing tautened and they were dragged under the sea. Marsden slashed at the rope with his jack-knife; it parted, and they were thrown to the surface. The dinghy was full of water now, flopping and swaying about; they couldn't see if it was leaking or simply waterlogged. The waves kept slopping over the gunwale; the water-level rose. They tried to bail the dinghy out, but it turned turtle—if they hadn't tied themselves to the safety lines they'd have been washed away. So they lay motionless, huddled together on the floor-boards. Their rubber immersion suits were supposed to be waterproof; but always the water found a way in. Soon they were wet and cramped and cold; wet and cramped and cold and sick. After a while Marsden remembered their drogue anchor. Moving very carefully he fished it out of its compartment and heaved it over the side. Almost at once the dinghy turned into wind and began to ride more easily.

They talked very little at first. Once the dinghy was under control, they checked their equipment; tested their mae-wests for inflation, and connected up their safety lights. Then, moving very carefully, they began to bail the dinghy out. For a while their movements kept the cold at bay; but after about ten minutes they felt a slow paralysis creeping over them, a gradual congealing of their blood. Marsden suggested they did exercises to keep up their circulation; and for several minutes they flexed their fingers and toes, and swung their arms as vigorously as they dared. But in spite of the exercises, their limbs soon lost all feeling; their movements became slow and clumsy and unco-ordinated. It was then that they began to talk—for they knew that if once they fell asleep they would never wake. But at last there came a time when neither movement nor conversation seemed possible, and they could only lie huddled together on the floor-boards. Round them the sea water began to turn to ice; and once they stopped moving the ice spread, spread over their immersion suits, then over their faces. Soon their eyes sealed up.

Marsden's observer kept getting little black-outs. One moment he was riding his piebald cob along the Devon lanes; the next, sea water would come slopping over his face. He would splutter and cough and spit it out, and then drift back into his world of dreams. After a while the moon broke through a rift in the clouds, carving a cross of silver in the sky. His head tilted up, as though he were considering the cross; but the eyes that turned skyward were sightless.

Marsden didn't notice for some time that his observer had died. Determined not to fall asleep, he had begun to crawl round and round the dinghy. He moved slowly, painfully, and with many lurches and falls. But he kept on. He wished his observer would get out of his way—it took so much extra effort to crawl over him. The fourth time round the dinghy he gave him a push and watched him fall stiffly to the floor-boards. He realized then that he was dead. A lesser man would have lost hope. But Marsden was not the sort to give up. He kept crawling on, round and round. His movements became slower. His pulse weakened; his brain reeled; but his body managed to retain a fragment of life-giving warmth.

He was crawling round the dinghy for the thirty-seventh time when *Dauntless* found him.

11

THE ships moved slowly eastward. In the narrows the sea was calmer; the wind had dropped, and soon the *aurora borealis* were rising over the northern horizon. Jardine watched the blue-green lights as they flickered above the pack ice. He hoped they weren't silhouetting the convoy; he hoped that somewhere to the south they weren't spotlighting *Dauntless* as she searched for the missing Swordfish. The destroyer had been gone for three hours now: too long.

Soon it was midnight. From the north came an occasional flash of silver—moonlight glinting on the ice. But from the south came no light; no message, only a sighing wind so gentle it scarcely ruffled the sea. I should never, Jardine thought, have let her go.

The ships moved silently on. The moon, reproachfully, hid behind a cloud.

After a while he moved to the other side of the bridge. He moved slowly, clumsily, as though uncertain of his balance, and when he got to the bridge rail he misjudged its distance and cannoned into the iron stanchions. The waves of tiredness were coming over him again, flooding in the more insistently for having been dammed back by the benzedrine. He swallowed two more tablets; and just as they were starting to take effect a look-out reported a light winking away in the south. It was *Dauntless* flashing her code letters.

'What luck?' Jardine signalled her, as a quarter of an

hour later the destroyer came swirling into the centre of the convoy.

'We have one survivor,' she flashed back. 'Name, Marsden.'

Through his tiredness the thankfulness welled up. The night seemed suddenly less cold. Marsden was a man worth saving.

The *aurora borealis* flickered and flared, weaved and weakened and died. The breeze faded to a sigh; the sea became flat as a prairie, and soon it was dawn. From the north, the pack ice began to close in, curving shoreward as the last eddies of the Gulf Stream were congealed to ice by contact with the arctic currents. To the south, the shoreline fell away, indented by a succession of ragged bays. On *Viper*'s radar screen the headlands of these bays stood out clearly; and behind the most easterly they could see their goal: Kola Bay, the last of the ice-free harbours, the gateway to Murmansk. This evening, thought Jardine, God and the tide willing, we'll be there.

The ships moved on, through waters that were motionless as glass. It was strangely quiet. A little after ten o'clock the sun heaved itself over the horizon. It was huge and evil and blood-red. Jardine had seen the sun rise like an ori-flamme out of the Bay of Bengal, and like an erupting volcano out of the Caribbean; but he had never seen it rise like this; as though it were trying to swallow the sky. Once it had lifted clear of the water it began to swell up, like an overblown balloon; even as he watched, he could see it expanding, spreading over the sky. Suddenly, it began to swing towards them.

He passed a hand over his forehead; his fingers came away wet. Around the carrier the sea began to tremble. A strange opaqueness filled the sky. Jardine looked at Agnew and saw that he was trembling. The Navigating Officer had gone dead white. The Yeoman was crossing himself.

Jardine snapped open a voice-pipe.

'MacLeod! On deck. Quickly.'

The sun was like a meteorite as MacLeod came tumbling

on to the bridge. It filled the eastern sky: a great circle of blood that men could stare into and feel no strain on their eyes, and reach for and feel no warmth on their hands. But the Met. Officer took only a single look at the sun. He looked instead at the sea, especially at the sea ahead of the carrier where little wisps of pearl-grey smoke were rising out of the water.

'Refracted light,' he said.

Agnew stopped trembling.

'Explain it simply,' said Jardine. 'Something I can pass on to the crew.'

'It's like his. Ye ken the water's ice-cuild. Well, the sun's warmin' it up. The change o' temperature is causin' sea-smoke to be drawn off. An' the smoke refracts an' magnifies the sun. An',' he added, 'the sea-smoke's thickenin'. Ye'd best be getting yon Swordfish back.'

It was true. Already visibility had dropped to the length of a soccer pitch; and as the whiteness thickened and the blood-red sun was blotted out, so one by one the ships of the convoy disappeared; first those that were far away, and then those that were near. There was something frightening about the way they were snuffed out—like used-up candles—as the sea-smoke rose swirling over them.

Lookouts were doubled. Navigation lights were shown. Radio silence was waived; and the convoy reverted to keeping station by radar.

Jardine looked at the rising miasma of grey.

'How long,' he asked, 'is it going to last?'

MacLeod scatched his head.

'I wouldn'a like tae say, sir. Maybe one hour. Maybe two.'

From overhead came the throb of an aircraft. The Swordfish was back, was searching for them in the swirling folds of grey. They listened as the engine-beat grew louder; it passed a little ahead of them, then it died away. She had missed them. A few minutes later they heard the beat again, moving slowly across their quarter; it echoed uncertainly among the spirals of sea-smoke; then for the second time it weakened and died.

Stone came clambering on to the bridge.

'Message from the Swordfish, sir. Their A.S.V.X. has died on them. The mist's blanketing the screen.'

'How long's she been airborne?'

'A couple of hours.'

'Tell her to circle us by D.R. plot. Until the mist clears.'

Halsey suggested they dropped magnesium flares to guide her in; but Jardine shook his head.

'Just what the U-boats would like,' he said.

The ships moved slowly forward. Above them circled the now useless Swordfish. For the first time since leaving the Shetlands the weather was good enough for U-boats to attack, and the convoy was without protection from the air. Undetected, the submarines closed in.

There were four of them: all that were left of the pack that had crossed swords with Jardine's escort the day before. They were hardly the barrier the Germans had hoped to string across Jardine's path; but they were at the right place, at the right time; and the sea-smoke came to their aid.

.　　　.　　　.　　　.　　　.

All sounds were muffled, muffled and distorted. Jardine could have sworn that the thud of depth-charges had come from astern; but the 'in contact' report came from a destroyer fine on their starboard bow. So even now, he thought, within sight of Kola Bay, they weren't yet out of the wood.

The blare of hooters brought *Viper's* off-duty watch on deck. The convoy dispersed to open formation. The ships began to zig-zag.

Again the depth-charges rumbled out, this time on their beam.

Jardine was hamstrung. His aircraft were useless. All he could do was wait for the mist to clear, and hope that for the next couple of hours his destroyers and corvettes could keep the U-boats at bay.

The U-boats didn't press their attacks home—they had tried that before; once bitten, twice shy. They hovered on the edge of the convoy, disappearing into the mist whenever a warship went after them. They launched their torpedoes discreetly, from extreme range. Out of the rising wreaths of sea-smoke the parallel ribbons of foam bore down on the convoy, aimed not at any particular ship but at the centre of the area of disturbance picked up by the submarines' hydrophones. And in the quiet water, hidden by the mist, many of them ran true.

'Torpedoes!'

First to sight them was a destroyer, guarding the convoy's flank. She swung head-on, and the foaming warheads flashed past her, two on either side. She fired starshell to illuminate their tracks; and the ships inside her saw them, and they too swung aside; and before the torpedoes reached the next column of merchantmen they sank.

But in their manœuvrings the ships got out of station; in the wreaths of sea-smoke they became confused. One of them, slow to revert to her original course, went yawing across the bows of the neighbouring column. The crew of a merchantman close to the convoy centre saw the sky to starboard suddenly darken. There were shouts of warning, cries of fear, as out of the swirling mist great bows came lowering towards them. The master flung his telegraph to stop, then to full astern. Slowly, her screws threshing the water, the merchantman shuddered to a halt; then even more slowly she began to back. And across her bow, less than a dozen feet away, swung the bulk of the errant merchantman. Before the master could think of a choice enough epithet to hurl at her, she had vanished into the mist.

'Torpedoes!'

This time it was a merchantman that spotted them first. Again the vessels swung and yawed aside; and again the torpedoes missed their mark. But the convoy became yet more disorganized, the ships wheeling and circling in the mist like a covey of disturbed partridge.

Jardine gritted his teeth. If this went on, sooner or later a merchantman would be hit. What was it he had sworn? No matter what else he lost, he'd not lose his merchantmen. He ordered a pair of destroyers to leave the convoy, to head straight for the U-boats, and in spite of the mist he ordered his last two Swordfish into the air.

The destroyers, as they pulled away from the convoy, knew what they had to do. They moved forward very slowly (their bows cutting the water with neither sound nor ripple) and very quietly (hoping the U-boats' hydrophones would fail to pick them up). Above them, distorted and half-hidden by the mist, hung the haloed disc of the sun: vast, blood-red and so near that it seemed as if the mast-head lookout could pluck it out of the sky. Around them rose the sea-smoke; phantom trails of white. The destroyers were both hunters and hunted. And they knew it: knew that as they stalked the U-boats, so the U-boats would be stalking them.

Soon, only a couple of miles from the fringe of the convoy, the leading destroyer was in contact. The ping of her Asdic echoing throughout the ship, she moved in silently to the attack. And just as silently another U-boat rose on her beam and launched a salvo of eight torpedoes. And hidden by the shrouds of sea-smoke they ran true.

The destroyer saw them too late. She tried to turn, but before she could swing head-on, the last of the salvo thudded into her about ten feet from her bow. She shuddered to a halt. A waft of pressurized air tore open her fo'c'sle, and she fell away, steam from her broken boilers rising skyward and mingling with the columns of mist. If she hadn't been moving slowly, and if the torpedo hadn't struck her obliquely, she would have sunk at once. As it was she stayed afloat, crippled and listing, while the second destroyer, coming up from astern, swept down on her attacker.

Depth-charges tore open the sea, and as the water subsided the crew of the second destroyer saw, spreading across the water, a widening patch of oil. It was heartening if inconclusive evidence. With other U-boats about they couldn't follow it up; but to judge from the amount of oil, one of the pack had been at least badly damaged. An eye for an eye, the destroyer captain thought as he headed back for his crippled colleague.

He found the first destroyer listing to twenty degrees, down by the bows, and 'blowing off' like a harpooned whale. But she was still under way, limping erratically among the rising columns of sea-smoke. The two ships circled each other, their signal lamps a-flicker.

They decided that the damaged destroyer was hit too badly to reach Murmansk. She would have to head for the entrance to Kola Bay; there, on the mud-flats of the Tuloma River, she would try to run aground.

She was now thirty miles from the entrance to the bay.

Alone, she would never have stood a chance; the U-boats would have followed her, would have pulled her down— as a wolf pack an injured bear. But the second destroyer stayed with her. Together the two ships dropped astern of the convoy. Together they steered a slow and painfully erratic course for the Tuloma estuary. And together they kept the U-boats at bay. Depth-charges patterned the sea, as again and again the undamaged destroyer drove their attackers off. Twice torpedoes were fired; but each time they missed by a hair's-breadth. And at last, baulked of an easy prey, the U-boats lost heart. Frustrated, they went back to the convoy.

The ships moved on, alone.

But soon the bows of the damaged destroyer sank even lower into the sea; her list increased; her speed dropped. Anxiously, her companion circled her, sending her encouraging signals. But signals couldn't dam the sea: the sea that flooded in faster than the pumps could pump it out. The destroyer's bow dropped even farther; soon she was barely under way.

It was about the time that the sea-smoke began to lift

that her fellow-destroyer took her in tow. And the tow-rope helped to keep her bow up. If the sea hadn't been a flat calm they would never have reached the shore. As it was, even through waters that were smooth as glass, it took them three hours to cover the last twenty miles.

It was dusk as the tow-rope was slipped. Quietly the damaged destroyer, continuing under way, slid with a sigh on to the Tuloma flats. The oozing mud sucked and plucked at her bows. She was held fast. Her crew waded ashore.

In the gathering darkness her fellow-destroyer left her. Moving quickly, while a faint sheen of daylight still lingered on the sea, she passed through the entrance to Kola Bay: the entrance through which, half an hour before, the ships of Jardine's convoy had filed in line ahead, silhouettes of ebony against a setting sun.

.   .   .   .   .

After the destroyer had been torpedoed the attacks on the convoy slackened off. Jardine's plan had worked: his sacrifice of the warships had not been in vain. For the U-boats now became divided, some following the merchantmen, others the destroyers. And once they had split up, their attacks lost weight, were easier to withstand. Soon, to add to their discomfort, the sea-smoke began to rise.

It rose with unexpected suddenness, the rays of the sun, as soon as they reached a certain temperature, sucking up the smoke like blotting-paper absorbing ink. Soon the ships were surrounded by rising columns of white that disappeared skyward like the tail-ends of ropes in the Indian rope trick. Through the mist the sky shone azure-blue; and in the sky were Jardine's Swordfish; and the U-boats had had more than enough of the Swordfish. They lacked the stomach for a last desperate assault. Faced again with a combined screen of warships and planes, they quietly submerged, and as quietly crept aside.

The way to Murmansk lay open.

Had the U-boats realized how thinly the forces opposing

them were stretched, they would have stayed to fight. But they had no means of knowing that the carrier, which for ten days had frustrated their every assault, had only three aircraft left. They went deep; and they didn't surface until it was dark.

Slowly, unmolested, the ships moved into Kola Bay.

Jardine looked at the Russian shoreline, now visible to the naked eye. So they were home at last. I ought, he thought, to be happy. Yet somehow happiness eluded him. Relief he felt, relief that the voyage was almost over. And thankfulness; thankfulness that of all his merchantmen not one had been lost through enemy action. That, he knew, was something to be proud of. But overshadowing every other feeling was his tiredness: the cramp in his legs, the blood-red haze in front of his eyes, and the fluttering of pinioned birds inside his brain. He felt the waves of faintness flooding over him again. He fought them off. Soon, he thought, I'll be able to sleep (and he knew he had never longed for anything quite so much); but not yet; not till we're inside the bay.

He turned *Viper* into wind, and two of his Swordfish came drifting down to land; the third plane he decided to keep airborne till they were inside the bay itself.

As the carrier swung round young Jardine clambered on to the batting platform. He too was tired, as tired as his father. Earlier that afternoon, as a point of interest, Stone had worked out how many planes he had landed-on since—ten days before—*Viper* had left the Shetlands. The total was three hundred and twenty-seven: forty planes a day: an average of nearly two an hour—yet the number of serious crashes could be counted on the fingers of a single hand. Even for two batsmen the strain of such a programme would have been near unendurable: for a single man it had been crippling. Now, for the three-hundred-and-twenty-eighth time, as the Swordfish drifted in, young Jardine keyed up his perceptions, and tautened his nerves. I mustn't, he thought, slacken off at the eleventh hour.

The first plane landed safely, thudding down dead

central, exactly opposite the batting platform. While it was being wheeled on to the lift and taken below, young Jardine paced the catwalk. From the opposite side of the flight deck the S.M.O. watched him carefully.

The second Swordfish came in off a long, especially careful, approach. In the dying moments of the convoy, everyone was making a conscious effort not to relax, not to fall victim to over-confidence. He held his bats level; and when the plane touched down safely, *Viper* herself seemed to sigh with relief. Now there was only one to come.

The carrier swung back into formation; the convoy moved slowly past the snow-white shore; the last A/S patrol circled overhead. By two o'clock the ships were very close to the entrance to Kola Bay.

Light was ebbing from the sky, when over the hills swept a formation of Mustangs and Aerocobras (American planes with Russian markings). They flew low over the convoy, their leader waggling his wings. And a few minutes later, fine on their starboard bow, a light started to wink; it was a Russian minesweeper, waiting to guide them in.

The sun was setting as they manœuvred to enter the bay. Its rays pricked out the ships in golden filigree as they filed through the headlands of the Tuloma Estuary: ahead the *Atalanta*; next the merchantmen, destroyers and corvettes; last the *Viper*. Sunlight slanted across the carrier's bridge. It hurt Jardine's eyes. He was only half conscious of what was happening around him: of the Senior Officers who were congratulating him; of the signals that were flooding in from the ships of his escort. He smiled and blinked and nodded as the bridge around him filled with chatter and bustle and laughter; and the bird in his brain fluttered madly and beat its pinioned wings.

'And we did it with so few losses,' he heard Agnew say.

The bird stopped its fluttering. Inside his head was a sudden silence, like the silence in a room where a clock that was ticking stops.

'No,' he said, 'our losses were heavy.'

Maitland and Sidwell, Green and Tewson, Ellis and Heywood and Blake: the names echoed inside his brain. He put a hand to his head, which felt suddenly empty. *Viper*'s flight deck began to undulate. A greyness covered his eyes, and he fell stiffly, like a man in an epileptic fit. Halsey caught him before he hit the deck.

They carried him below and laid him out on his bunk. The S.M.O. took his pulse and loosened his clothing; then he found, in the pocket of his oilskins, the bottle of benzedrine tablets. I wonder, he thought, how many he's taken? He spent the best part of half an hour in Jardine's cabin. When he left him the Captain was in his pyjamas and asleep, and likely to remain that way for all of forty-eight hours. The doctor knew that clinically speaking there was nothing seriously the matter with him—though what the long-term effect of so much cumulative strain would be, time alone would tell. He looked round the cabin. Jardine's writing-desk was open, and inside it a photograph of his son lay on its side, sticking out of a pigeon-hole. The doctor picked it up. A good likeness, he thought. He stood the photograph on a table at the side of the Captain's bunk.

.   .   .   .   .

Once they were inside the bay, Agnew ordered the last of their Swordfish to land-on. *Viper* turned into wind, and as the rest of the convoy passed down-river to Vaengar—the port of Murmansk—the carrier waited for her final plane.

An evening breeze was blowing offshore, going out with the tide. The light was grey, the waves were smooth and oily. It was very quiet.

Young Jardine held his bats at 'steady', as out of the twilight the plane came drifting in. She came in smoothly, carefully, off a shallow descending turn. Soon she was level with the round-down, poised over the carrier's stern. Jardine took a half step forward. Another fraction of a second and he'd have given the pilot the signal to cut. His wrists dropped as he started to swing down the bats. Then on the back of his neck he felt a blast of hot air, accompanied by the smell of burning oil. He knew what would happen next.

The Swordfish flickered as though caught in an air pocket; her port wingtip dropped; she slewed sideways; she came lurching straight for the batting platform.

It had all happened before.

A cry of fear rose thinly into the night. The men in the catwalk flung themselves to the deck. Young Jardine didn't have time to think. He acted by instinct. He took a pace backward and waved the Swordfish to starboard, trying desperately in the fraction of a second left him to align her centrally with the deck. And the pilot saw his signal. With a last-second flick of aileron and rudder he wrenched the plane level; and she landed safely—safely but on the very edge of the flight deck. Her wingtip swept at seventy miles an hour over the face of the batting platform.

Young Jardine leapt aside. But he wasn't quite in time. The lower wing smashed into the padded shoulder of his flying jacket, and he was spun toppling into the safety net.

For a second he lay spreadeagled among the yielding strands of netting. He was more shocked than stunned. Then he remembered the Swordfish. Scrambling to his feet, he saw that the plane had been jerked to a stop on the very extremity of the deck. The pilot and observer were tumbling out, unhurt. But it had been a near thing.

Before anyone had had time to recover from the shock, the Deck Officer was scurrying about the flight deck, asking questions, making notes. As soon as he had collected all the information he needed he hurried below, and in the quiet of his cabin sat down to write his official report. For now at last he had all the facts, all the evidence.

'*To their Lords Commissioners,*' he began, '*a report is enclosed on the landing operations aboard* H.M.S. Viper *between December 2nd and December 13th, 1944. . . .*' There followed a detailed analysis of the four occasions during their passage to

Murmansk when an aircraft approaching to land had drifted suddenly, inexplicably, and on two occasions fatally, to port. Then came the kernel of what he had to say.

'*Each time that an accident took place, the wind was light and swinging from dead ahead to fifteen degrees on the starboard bow; also on each occasion the carrier was steaming at* 14 *knots. In order to maintain this speed it is common practice among Engineer Officers to set the engine revolution counters to "normal full" which gives a speed of* 14.05 *knots; the excess speed is then compensated for by the periodic idling of the engines.*

'*It is submitted that the cause of the accidents was as follows. With the carrier travelling at* 14 *knots, the engines would be subjected to occasional sudden increases in tempo, following the periods of idling. On these occasions there would naturally be a sudden discharge of fumes from the port vents.[1] These fumes would be hot, would smell of burnt oil and would leave the vents in the form of a current of warm air. Under normal conditions this current would be swept directly astern of the carrier; but with the wind swinging from about ten or fifteen degrees on the starboard bow, it would be swept directly into the path of an aircraft approaching to land. An aircraft flying close to its stalling speed and being struck by such a current would naturally become out of control.*'

The Deck Officer filled another couple of pages with comments and suggestions. He was glad he had collected so conclusive a weight of evidence; glad he hadn't discussed his theory before he was able to substantiate it. He signed his report with a flourish. This, he felt sure, had been the right way to do things; this way all the credit would fall where it was most deserved. On himself.

.　　　.　　　.　　　.　　　.

Young Jardine sat on his batting platform watching the stars swing one by one into a velvet sky. He wanted to keep awake until *Viper* had dropped anchor inside Vaengar boom.

[1] These vents are the carrier's funnels, built into the superstructure below and a little aft of the bridge.

The flight deck was deserted now; the barrier was lowered; the safety nets were furled. It was the end of the voyage. It was the end too of other things: of his uncertainty and fear and foolish pride. He was at peace with himself at last. He knew that when the final Swordfish had come side-slipping on top of him, he hadn't had time to think; he hadn't had time to reason 'Now this is what I must do'; he had acted instinctively. Courage had come to him as if it had been his birthright. Yet he hadn't always been brave. That he knew. It was the convoy that had made him that way.

He settled himself more comfortably against the bridge-rail, and watched the shore drift slowly past: low, snow-covered hills less than a couple of miles away. Between the ship and the shore the tide was ebbing fast: tumbling, luminous and phosphorescent. He looked at it and shivered. When the war's over, he thought, I'll never come back to the sea. Never again.

He wondered if he ought to go below to see his father; but the physical effort of getting up was more than he felt capable of. He suddenly realized that the thought of his father no longer brought any terror with it. No longer need he struggle to prove and justify himself. What his father thought of him no longer mattered. For now he knew himself, knew what manner of man he was, and saw in himself nothing of which he need be ashamed. As a snake sloughs off its skin, he left behind at that moment all the years of hero-worship and make-believe and imitation. He was a man at last.

He sat hunched up on his batting platform, watching the sea and the shore and the sky. In his mind was a pool of sleep, a pool he had managed for the last eight days to keep dammed back. But now quite suddenly the pool broke its banks, tiredness came flooding over him, and he slumped sideways against the deck-rail, fast asleep.

Down in his cabin Captain Jardine also slept, the photograph of his son beside his bed.

In single file the ships moved slowly upriver. Soon they

came to the boom at the entrance to Vaengar harbour; once inside they dropped anchor. Their battles too were over. Above them the sky was silent with stars; around them the water was motionless as sleep. Now, at the end of the voyage, they and all aboard them could rest at last.

© Hutchinson & Co. (*Publishers*) Ltd. 1958